The Case of the
Curious Canine

MW01076283

The Samantha Wolf Mysteries
#7

TARA ELLIS

ISBN-13: 978-1541020078
ISBN-10: 1541020073

The Case of the Curious Canine

Cover art design Copyright © Melchelle Designs
http://melchelle.designs.com/

Models: Breanna Dahl, Janae Dahl, Chloe Hoyle
Schnoodle: Daisy, Poodle: Baxter, Great Dane: Gracie
Photographer: Tara Ellis Photography

AUTHOR'S NOTE

I found my first best friend at the pound at the age of four. Her name was Pepper, and she was a small, white terrier mix that was smarter than I probably ever realized. There have been numerous others over the years, and I currently have two furry kids named Daisy and Baxter (pictured on the cover).

While thinking about Sam, Ally, and the rest of the kids and the type of new adventure they could get into in their small town of Oceanside, I realized that something was missing. None of the stories had a dog in it! That had to change.

So this particular book is dedicated to Pepper. She taught me one of my first lessons about unconditional love and I will never, ever forget her.

Samantha Wolf Mysteries

CONTENTS

1

A CHARITY TO SINK YOUR FANGS INTO

Samantha Wolf peddles hard to keep up with her best friend, Allyson Parker. The air is crisp since it's only late February and spring is still a month away. The one snowfall from their unusual Christmas storm is long gone, replaced by brown, crunchy grass and old, decaying leaves. Sam always finds this time of year to be depressing here, in the Pacific Northwest. Their hometown of Oceanside is nestled along the Washington State shoreline, and has many positive things to boast, but the late winter weather is *not* one of them.

Hopefully, this afternoon will lift all of our moods!

Sam thinks, looking up from the mesmerizing colors rushing under her tires, to study her two closest friends.

Ally and Cassy are both bundled up in their thick winter coats, but it's still easy to tell the two apart. Cassy is nearly as tall as Sam is, but not quite as solidly built. She inherited her long black hair and olive skin from her Hispanic father, a stark contrast to Ally's bright red hair and lighter, freckled skin. Ally is also the shortest of the duo, and rather slim.

Sam reminds herself to ask Ally to stay for dinner later, when they get back from their new Sunday afternoon job. Well, it's not technically a job because they aren't old enough at twelve, and aren't being paid. But Cassy's older sister, Lisa Covington, assured them that it would be a lot of work volunteering at the local animal shelter. Lisa's friend, Mrs. Spartan, is the manager of the shelter, and asked her for help. Since Lisa has several horses to take care of now at her family ranch she's been renovating, she asked the girls if they could go, instead.

The girls recently created a successful club at their middle school, where they select a different charity each month and then raise money for them. They immediately added the shelter to their list, but there's already several other needy groups ahead of them. This month, they're putting on a bake sale, and they hope to raise enough to purchase some new mattresses for a local woman's shelter.

October was the first month they formed the club, with the help of Lisa Covington, who aside from being Cassy's sister is also their Physical Education teacher. The haunted house they built was a hit. In December they collected, wrapped, and delivered presents to families who might have otherwise not had any.

Sam, Ally, Cassy, and a handful of other students have been surprised at how fun the fundraising has been. Even their older brothers, John, and Hunter, have gotten in on some of the projects. In fact, today they're supposed to be going over their recipes and making out the shopping lists for ingredients. Since John can drive, he offered to take them grocery shopping. When Lisa approached them yesterday about going to the shelter, they all agreed to do it and will have to manage the shopping sometime afterschool this next week, instead.

Puffing a little harder as she struggles up a hill, Sam tries not to get too stressed out over the details. Mrs. Spartan said that she's suddenly short-handed on Sunday's, so that's the only day they're committing to. Besides, it's bound to be fun working with the animals.

"We're almost there!" Ally gasps, looking back over her shoulder at Sam.

"Come on, slowpoke!" Cassy teases. "I think that you've been eating too many of the cookie samples, Sam!"

Sam laughs at her friends joke, because Cassy is notoriously the biggest eater of the three. She even rivals Sam's brother, Hunter. At fourteen, he's a food-machine, but Cassy keeps up with him whenever she's over for dinner. Sam has no idea how her friend does it.

Unable to turn down a challenge, Sam pushes harder and passes both of her friends. As they barrel around a curve, the road deposits them into the downtown area of the small city. Traffic is light, being a Sunday, and they're able to spread out across the street.

"Isn't it a couple of blocks that way?" Ally

asks, pointing to their left.

"Yup!" Sam confirms. Sticking her arm out straight to signal a left-hand turn, she speeds up again. This roadway is narrow, so they're forced to ride single file in the small space between the fog line and sidewalk.

Sam is quite familiar with the shelter. Although it's been several years, she'll never forget the time that her dad took her there. They'd found a poor, miserable dog outside their house. Sam, of course, had wanted to keep it but unfortunately, her brother Hunter is extremely allergic. It was even worse once inside the shelter and Sam saw all of the other dogs and cats lined up in cages. She cried when they handed the German Shepard over, and persisted for the rest of the night. Her parents haven't taken her back since.

Her mom questioned the wisdom behind her subjecting herself to so many needy animals, knowing that she can't bring any of them home. Sam's defense is that she's much older now, and that she'll be able to handle it. However, as Sam sees the distinct building come into view, the faint stirring of anxiety low in her belly challenges that notion.

2

LEARNING THE ROPES THE SPARTAN WAY

The bell over the door chimes as the three girls enter, announcing their arrival.

"Thank goodness you're here!"

Turning towards the source of the pleasant voice, Sam discovers a plump, middle-aged woman hustling towards them. Her chestnut-colored hair is pulled up in a loose bun that is falling apart, and the front of her blue t-shirt looks soaking wet. It's likely due to the dripping, trembling Chihuahua cradled in her arms. Based on both of their expressions, the bath must have been a harrowing experience.

"Are we late?" Ally asks, worried that they

already made a mistake.

"No!" Mrs. Spartan is quick to correct. "It's just that we had a couple of new intakes first-thing this morning, and then Simba here decided to roll in something he discovered in the backyard.

Sam grins at the totally unsuitable name for the tiny dog, and steps forward with arms outstretched. "I can take Simba," she offers. "Do you have a drier I can put him under?"

Looking relieved, the shelter director gladly hands him over. "It's an ancient contraption, but it still gets the job done," she states, already walking towards the back of the main entrance area.

Sam scrambles to keep up, while trying to contain the unhappy dog. It's a good thing she didn't take her coat off, so at least her clothes won't get wet. Ally and Cassy are quick to follow, and they all crowd into a room that is obviously set up as the bathing area. Two large sinks are set against the back wall. To one side are a double row of stacked cages, while the opposite wall to their right has a grooming station, complete with a suspended leash and portable dryer.

Sam makes a beeline for the dryer, and figures out on her own how to position the dog in it. He seems frightened when she first turns it on, but soon the warm air lures the canine into a peaceful sort of trance.

Nodding her approval at Sam's initiative, Mrs. Spartan steps forward to make the formal introductions. "I'm Mrs. Spartan, the 'leader' around here," she says good-humoredly, speaking loudly to be heard over the dryer. "You all should just call me Trish. It makes conversations easier." Winking, she extends a hand to Sam first.

"Nice meet you," Sam replies, taking the offered hand. "My name is Samantha Wolf, but everyone calls me Sam." She isn't surprised to find Trish's grip solid. The older woman instantly reminds Sam of her Aunt Beth, her mother's sister. Aunt Beth and Uncle Bill own a mansion in Montana that they have renovated into an inn. Aunt Beth is the sort of person that says it like it is, and Sam has the distinct feeling that Trish is the same way.

"I'm Allyson Parker."

Trish beams at Ally, and places her hands on her hips after an equally firm shake. "My goodness, look at that hair!" she exclaims. "I haven't seen that gorgeous hue of red since my sister!"

When Ally's smile falters, uncertain whether to feel insulted or complimented, Trish waves a hand. "Don't take that the wrong way, Ally. I hold redheads in the highest regard. When I was little, I was tormented by the fact that my younger sister was blessed with something so beautiful, while I was fated to be simply ordinary."

As she turns to focus her energy onto Cassy, Sam and Ally exchange a look behind Trish's back. After a brief pause, they both smile wide. It's clear that their time at the shelter is going to be immensely entertaining.

"That must mean that you're Cassy, the long-lost sister of my long-lost friend, Lisa Covington."

Lisa grew up in Oceanside, but moved to go live with her aunt after both her parents were tragically killed in a plane crash when she was sixteen. It wasn't until recently that she came back to work as a teacher at their middle school and to rescue the family ranch, which had fallen into disrepair. With the help of Sam and Ally, Lisa also discovered that she'd been adopted be her parents and that her unknown half-sister, Cassy, lived in the same town with her ailing grandmother.

The moving story is now widely known amongst the residents of Oceanside, and Cassy is used to the attention that it brings her. She reaches out to accept the greeting without missing a beat, and laughs at Trish's play on words. She was rather shy, before meeting Ally and Sam, but their solid friendship helped bring out the *real* Cassy.

"The one and only!" Cassy jests, pulling her hand back to make a mock-salute. "Here and ready to do your bidding!"

"We are going to get along *very* well," Trish replies. "At ease, and march this way!"

Cassy does a sloppy about-face, and follows Trish through another doorway off the grooming room. Sam snatches up the almost-dry dog, earning her a rather irritated look from the Chihuahua. Hugging him close, she whispers an apology to him before scrambling after Ally.

A short hallway opens up into a massive

room that takes up nearly the entire back half of the building. It's lined with varying sized kennels and cages, and as soon as Trish pushes open the heavy door leading to it, the noise inside is deafening.

Sam's eyes begin to sting with unshed tears, as she examines the dozen or so dogs behind bars. Ranging in size from a large Rottweiler to a tiny puppy, they're all equally sad-looking.

"Here, this is Simba's abode," Trish tells Sam, directing her to one of the smaller containers near them.

As Sam sets the shaking dog inside, a lone tear spills over and she tries to wipe it away unnoticed. But as she suspected, nothing much gets past Trish.

"Are you going to be able to handle this, Sam?" she asks softly, placing a hand on Sam's shoulder. "I know that this is shocking and a little tough, but we really are helping them. This is a no-kill shelter, which means that we take care of these guys until we find them a good forever home. No one gets left behind."

Sniffing, Sam carefully considers Trish's words. Looking again at the various dogs she notes how they all appear clean, well fed, and healthy. The thought that she and her friends can help care for them and take them out for walks and play with them, is enough to push aside her sadness.

Standing a little straighter, Sam looks at Trish confidently. "Yes, I think I'll be fine," she assures her. "It's just been a long time since I saw an animal in a cage. But I know we're here to help them, and I would love to be a part of that!"

Smiling now, Trish claps her hands together. "Well, then! Let's get on with it."

But before she can continue, a young girl walks into the room. She doesn't look any older than nineteen and her long dark hair is pulled back into a functional ponytail.

"Trish! I have someone up front with a cat that was just pulled out from under their house. I think it's okay, but I figured I better have you take a look before accepting it, to make sure it doesn't need a vet. Oh, and they also said that they're looking for their neighbor's dog. A little white, girl Schnauzer. I haven't seen one of those in a long time, though."

"Pauline, meet our new volunteers: Sam, Ally,

and Cassy. Girls," Trish says, turning back to them, "this is Pauline, one of only two other employees. She's a first-year student at the local college, where she's working towards becoming a vet." Facing Pauline again, she then waves at the cages. "Why don't you introduce them to all our friends while I go deal with the trespassing feline?"

Trish marches from the room before Pauline even has a chance to respond, leaving the four girls to stare at each other expectantly.

"Umm … hi, nice to meet you," Pauline says a bit awkwardly. "It'll be nice to have some more help. I'm not even full-time. I can't be, with my classes and all. Trish has been doing pretty much everything on her own, since Craig quit last weekend. He was normally in charge on Saturday and Sunday, and was on-call for emergencies during the week. She has one other volunteer with her Monday through Friday, but that's it. I think Trish is hoping that between the four of us, we can cover the weekend work."

"Does that mean you'll be here by yourself on Saturdays?" Ally asks, concerned.

"Yeah, but its fine," Pauline says. "I can

handle all the normal feeding and such; it's just that Sundays are when we usually do all the grooming and deep cleaning of the kennels. That's too much work for one person."

"Hasn't Trish been able to hire a replacement for the guy that quit?" Ally asks, hoping she isn't being too nosey.

"No, and she isn't going to," Pauline explains, seemingly unbothered by the question. "The city just raised our rent starting at the first of the year. Then Craig *demanded* a raise, the same week that Trish found out one of our contributors doesn't have the funds to donate anymore. She had to tell Craig no, and so he got mad and quit. Personally, I say good riddance. He was lazy. He acted like his degree in biology made him better than us, but he didn't have a way with the animals. Still … it'll be hard to replace him when we can't pay for it."

"Well, don't worry!" Cassy states, stepping forward. "We're happy to help and we're hard workers. I'd love to meet all the animals. Do you have any cats?"

Laughing, Pauline looks relieved. "We sure do, but we keep them in a separate room for obvious reasons. Come on," she adds, heading for yet another door at the far end of the dog kennel area. "We'll start there. We have this amazing cat named Yoda that you have to see to believe."

Falling in behind the friendly teen, Sam reaches out to pet a random dog in passing. As the cute little mixed breed licks at her hand, Sam is reassured that the donated afternoons are going to be well worth it.

3

BABYSITTING BLUES

"I wanna cookie!"

Sam tries to ignore the little girl pulling at her arm, but Cora is very persistent. The five-year-old lives across the street from Ally, and her mom asked the girls if they could watch her tonight because she has to work late. Since Sam and Ally live only one house away from each other, they are usually at each other's homes and end up doing practically everything together.

The daycare Cora goes to during the week is within walking distance, so it was easy for them to go check her out at five, and bring her back to Ally's house. Since it's Friday, they have plans with Cassy for a sleepover, and are hoping to catch up on the bake sale organizing. However, it's nearly eight, and Cora's mom *still* hasn't shown up. She's a single parent and doesn't have anyone else to rely on.

"Cora, you know your mommy doesn't want you to have another treat this late," Sam says reasonably. Cora doesn't see the wisdom and instantly begins to howl, throwing herself on the floor of the rec room. Unfazed by the tantrum, Sam just stares solemnly at the blond curls thrashing around on the ground. She has twin sisters that turn three in a few weeks, so this is nothing.

"Make it stop!" Hunter shouts from across the large room. He's been playing a game of foosball with Ally's sixteen-year-old brother, John. The two are best friends in spite of their age difference.

The boys eagerly agreed to be taste testers for a couple of recipes the girls were going to bake tonight. With the unplanned babysitting job, all they've gotten so far are some sugar cookies that Cassy brought with her when she arrived after dinner.

Sam glares at her brother, irritated that he has

enough nerve to complain, when he's been able to spend the night playing games, instead of chasing the energetic five-year-old around the large house.

"I'm with Hunter on this one," Cassy interjects from her perch on the sofa, where she is watching the intense match between the teens. "Just give her a cookie. We won't be the ones up with her tonight!" For emphasis, she plucks a cookie from the bowl nestled in her lap and tosses it at Sam. True to her reputation, Cassy already ate several of them herself, while doling the stash out to Hunter and John.

Snatching the treat from the air, Sam quickly hides it in her palm before Cora sees it. "That would be reinforcing horrible behavior," Sam counters. But hearing her, Cora begins to scream even louder, and Sam's confidence wavers. *Maybe just this once,* she thinks, looking at the cookie.

Before she has a chance to give in, there's a loud knock at the front door.

"Thank goodness. That has to be Cora's mom!" Ally cries out while jumping up and running for the foyer.

Her dad gets there first and pulls the door

wide, inviting Kendra Pierce inside. Ally's mom is still at work at the hospital where she's a nurse, and in charge of the Intensive Care department. The two adults exchange pleasantries before her dad retreats back to his study.

Hearing her daughter wailing in the other room, Kendra's looks at Ally apologetically. "I'm so sorry; I just couldn't get away from work any sooner. Has she been like this all night?"

"No, she's been fine!" Ally reassures her. "She just started. We wouldn't give her another cookie. She already had two and we were afraid you wouldn't approve."

Visibly relaxing, Kendra fishes around in her purse before pulling out a ten-dollar bill. "Well, you have no idea how much I appreciate this," she says, looking at Sam as she enters the foyer, leading a still-sniffing Cora by the hand. "Oh!" she exclaims, quickly giving the money to Ally before opening her purse again. "I need to pay you too, Sam."

Sam studies the white lab coat that the young mother is wearing, which reaches her knees and has a large patch on the front with the letters sTb centered in it. Sam's never thought to ask what her job is, but now she's curious. There are large smears of what appears to be dirt on the coat, as well as wet blotches. When Kendra looks up from her purse and meets Sam's gaze, she's shocked to see the obvious signs of a recent, hard cry. Kendra's eyes are red rimmed and puffy, and her fair complexion is marred by spots of redness, especially around her nose and lips. What could have happened?

"You don't need to give me anything, Ms. Pierce," Sam declares, when she realizes that Kendra is holding money out to her. Waving it off, she instead ushers Cora forward. "We're happy to help out anytime."

Any further argument is stopped by Cora, who promptly throws herself at her mother. "Mommy!" she cries, hugging her legs.

Kneeling down, Kendra gathers the little girl into her arms. "Are you tired, Angel? We'll go home now and finish the book we started last night, okay?"

Nodding, Cora cheers up instantly. "With the pirates?" She asks, hopping up and down eagerly.

"You bet!" But as Kendra goes to stand, Cora suddenly starts to cough and looks at her mother with wide eyes.

"What's wrong?" Ally asks. She's concerned about the raspy breathing suddenly taking over the little girl.

"Allergies," Kendra replies flatly, already yanking off her lab coat in disgust. "How could I be so stupid? I was in such a rush, that I didn't leave my jacket at the lab!" Dropping the dirty garment to the floor, she then whips an inhaler from her purse.

Sam recognizes the device immediately, because Hunter has one, too. He usually only needs to use the rescue inhaler when he's sick and his lungs get tight enough that it's hard for him to breathe. The doctor diagnosed him with mild asthma last year.

Shaking the palm-sized, L-shaped medication dispenser, Kendra then holds the open end to Cora's lips. "Ready?" she asks. "One, two, three --" As Cora takes a big breath; Kendra pushes down on the top of the inhaler, dispensing the medication as an aerosol into Cora's lungs. They've undoubtedly done this many times before.

The little girl's eyes are huge as she looks at

her mother while holding her breath. After a moment, Kendra gives her a nod and she releases the trapped air. Cora's next breath is markedly clearer, and the coughing seems to have stopped.

Holding her daughter by the shoulders, Kendra then places an ear next to her chest and listens as she breathes. "Okay," she announces, smiling. "I think you only need the one puff this time, angel. Let's go home."

A little shaken by the event, Sam and Ally hold onto each other silently and watch as Kendra and Cora wave goodbye.

"Wait!" Ally suddenly calls out, while grabbing the lab coat off the floor. Running to the still-open door, she holds it up. "What do you want me to do with this? We can wash it for you, if you'd like."

Hesitating at the end of the driveway, Kendra Pierce studies the garment for a moment with squinted eyes. "No," she decides, shaking her head. "Throw it away."

4

THE LOVE OF A DOG

The bell out front chimes, and Sam looks up from where she's doing her best to wash a dog. It isn't going very well. Someone who found it along the side of the road brought the poor thing in the night before. Pauline's main concern at that time had been for its health. Due to the condition of its skin, she'd called in the vet, afraid that it might have mange, which is a parasitic infection. Pauline explained how mites get into their skin and eventually can lead to sores and the hair falling out in patches.

The Veterinarian cleared it of anything infectious, and figures it's severe allergies. Probably due to the food she's been fed. Sam's first assignment when they arrived at the shelter was to clean her up. She's a sweet little thing and as the dirt, mud, and grime are washed down the drain, she's surprised to discover that what they thought was a brown dog is actually white!

Sam can hear Pauline out front talking with whoever entered the building. Ally and Cassy are still out on a walk with two of the larger dogs, who need the most exercise. Fortunately, there is a perfect, wooded trail nearby.

Sam is placing her charge into the dryer when Pauline returns, holding a new intake out at arm's length. It looks like a miniature poodle, but it's condition is similar to the other dog. Maybe even worse.

"Here, Sam," Pauline directs, approaching her. "I'll take over the drying while you get to work on this miserable guy."

Miserable is a good word for him. What should be springy, curly, cinnamon colored fur is instead matted together in clumps by dirt and mud. Patches of bare, raw skin are visible on his hindquarters and his chocolate colored eyes are red and inflamed. As he looks up forlornly at Sam, their eyes meet for the first time and her heart goes out to him.

"Some kids found him in a field," Pauline explains, setting him in Sam's arms.

He's not a small dog at around 25 lbs., but still light enough for her to easily hold him. He immediately snuggles in under her chin, and Sam doesn't even care how dirty he's getting her.

Turning to carry him over to the sink, Sam suddenly stops. Spinning back towards Pauline, she stares intently at the now-white dog.

"What is it?" Pauline asks, a little alarmed. "I don't think we have to worry about mange. It looks like the same sort of allergic reaction."

"No," Sam replies, shaking her head. "It's not that. I just realized something. Isn't that a Schnauzer?" she asks, pointing an elbow towards the little dog. When Pauline nods, Sam breaks out in a wide smile. "Last Sunday when we were here, wasn't there a couple who brought in a cat? I thought you said that they were looking for a white, female Schnauzer."

"Sam!" the older girl exclaims. "You're brilliant! I think you're right. I'll go look up their information and call them as soon as she's done drying. Good job!"

Beaming with pride at the compliment, Sam hurries to the wash station. Gently setting the poodle in the sink, she slowly gets him accustomed to the water temperature the way that Pauline showed her. She discovered that morning that there's a lot more to it than she realized. Methodically going back over all the steps in her head, she then begins the process.

Ten minutes later, he's looking more like a poodle, but has begun to shake. Speaking to him in a calm, sing-song voice, Sam does her best to ease his fear. "You're a handsome boy, aren't you? Yes, you are. Look at all this gorgeous, red hair!"

Turning his head slightly, he stares at her curiously. His shaking has stopped.

"You like that?" she asks, gently rubbing at the space between his floppy ears. In response, the dog closes his eyes and leans back into her hand. "What happened to you?" Sam murmurs, while continuing his doggy massage under the warm, running water. "I can tell you're a fighter. Aren't you? You might get knocked down, but you'll get right back up again. Just like Rocky!" At the mention of the name, the dogs eyes spring back open and he tenses slightly under her hands.

"What? do you like that name?" Sam asks, smiling at him. He stares back with such unwavering intensity that Sam almost expects him to answer. She's never sensed so much intelligence in a dog before. "Rocky?" she repeats, unable to break away from his gaze.

Whimpering slightly, the poodle shuffles his feet and licks at his lips, obviously interested in the game they seem to be playing. It almost looks like he's smiling now.

"Okay," Sam says with more resolution. "Rocky it is! How about we get you out of this sink, Rocky?"

Settling back on his haunches, he then stands up as soon as Sam turns the water off, placing his paws against her shoulders. Laughing now, Sam first drapes a towel around him and then gathers him up. She laughs even harder when he scoots his back paws to either side of her waist so that she's left holding him like a baby. Poodles are one of the breeds with unique hip joints so that you can hold them in this manner, although Sam doesn't know if it's a recommended practice to do so.

"It looks like you've made a friend!" Pauline observes.

Bringing 'Rocky' over to the dryer, they swap the two dogs out. While the dogs cautiously sniff at each other, the two seem to be willing to get along.

"There you go, Rocky. It's okay, it's just warm air!"

Pauline looks curiously at Sam. "Rocky?" she asks, eyebrows raised.

Blushing slightly, Sam shuffles her feet. "Is it okay to give him a name? He seems to like it."

Laughing, Pauline scoops the little Schnauzer up. "No, I don't mind at all. Just be careful," she cautions. "It's way too easy to get attached."

Looking down at Rocky, Sam wonders if Pauline is right. But when the poodle responds to her gaze by licking her hand, any misgivings melt away.

5

STRANGE BEHAVIOR

Sam thumps the cover closed on her math book. "Done!" she announces.

Ally looks up from her history book, the skepticism clear on her face. "Did you re-do the assignment from yesterday, too?"

The two of them are sitting on Sam's bed, hidden away in her room from both her brother and twin sisters. Her mom promised them some peace and quiet for at least an hour, so they can finish their homework. They're due up at Cassy's house, Covington Ranch, before dinner. Lisa invited them over for both food *and* planning time for the bake sale. They've fallen even further behind in their schedule. They're supposed to have the sale this coming weekend but that's beginning to seem nearly impossible. They still need to finalize the recipes and purchase all the ingredients. Then make flyers, advertise, bake, and then set it up in the school auditorium Saturday.

Between school and volunteering at the shelter, they're all spread thin. And Sam hasn't been able to stop thinking about Rocky, wondering if his owners have come to claim him yet. Pauline doesn't think that's likely to happen, because yet another dog with the same symptoms came in right before the girls left for the evening. The older girl thinks that someone has been collecting strays and perhaps feeding them bad food. The schnauzer's owners were thrilled to see her, but horrified by her condition. They swore she had been fine just ten days before, the last time they saw her.

"Sam? Did you do it all?" Ally repeats, the crease between her brows deepening.

Trying to concentrate, Sam pushes her book away and huffs in response. "I got today's assignment done. I only have ten equations to do over," she rushes to explain, trying to cut off her friends reprimand. "I can do that tomorrow before class."

"Sam, it was really nice of Mr. Cooper to even give you the option of doing the assignment over. You *know* you need all the extra points you can get!"

Sam studies the digital clock on her nightstand. It's only 3:40. Ally is right. She can spend another ten or fifteen minutes on her homework before they go. If her grade falls any further in math, she's sure to get grounded. Picking the pencil back up, she flips the textbook open without a word.

Less than five minutes later, Ally's cellphone rings. "Hi, Ms. Pierce," she answers after looking at the display to see who it is. Listening for a minute, she frowns for the second time that evening. "Sure. I can help out. Would it be okay if I take Cora up to my friend's house at Covington Ranch? Oh. That's right. Yes, they have several horses and I think an outdoor barn cat. All right …. Yes, I'll still do it."

Hanging up, Sam and Ally look at each other silently for a moment. It's obvious that yet again, their plans have been derailed.

"I'm sorry," Ally says softly. "I just couldn't say no, Sam. She seemed upset again. With Cora's allergies, Ms. Pierce is afraid to have her around the animals." Ally hates to disappoint her friends, and is normally the one everyone can rely on the most.

"It's only Tuesday," Sam replies. "I'm sure that Cassy and I can at least get the lists put together tonight. John said he could take us shopping Thursday night, so we'll be able to get all the baking done Friday with the help of Cassy's Aunt Clara, and Lisa."

"What about the flyers?" Ally questions, looking dejected.

"Maybe you can make some up on your computer tonight while you're watching Cora?" Sam suggests. "Give Cora some paper and crayons and pretend like she's helping!"

Laughing at the brilliant scheme, Ally cheers up. "That's a great idea, Sam! I'll bet John will help me out. He's a wiz with some of the programs and designs. He had to make a brochure for one of his classes last year."

Encouraged, Sam looks again at the clock and discovers that it's now time to go. "I need to head out before it starts getting dark." Covington Ranch is only a couple of miles away but it's up a fairly steep, wooded hill that takes some work on a bike. It still gets dark out early this time of year, and night comes even sooner in the forest. Lisa Covinton will give her a ride home later. She has a work truck at the ranch and they can toss her bike in the back.

Ally silently gathers her things in response, and then briefly hugs her best friend. "Text me when you guys figure out the final list for the desserts we're going to make," she instructs while swinging her backpack over a shoulder. "I might already have some of the ingredients so we won't have to buy it all.

Nodding, Sam then follows Ally out of her room and tells her goodbye. Pausing in the family room where her mom is playing an intense game of catch with Tabitha and Addison, Sam studies her little sisters for a moment. Nearly three, they both have the same naturally curly, blond waves as their mother. Hunter and Sam inherited their own dark hair from their dad. While the twins also have their moms blue eyes, and Hunter his dad's brown, Sam ended up with the unlikely color of green. No one claims to know which side of the family it comes from.

The thoughts of her dad dampen Sam's mood. He's a commercial fisherman and is up in Alaska right now, in charge of what he claims is an amazing Cod season. He used to only be gone for one or two different seasons a year, but since he was promoted, he's been in Alaska fishing for nearly six months straight! He was able to come home over Christmas, but then went back last month.

"Leaving for Cassy's?" Kathy Wolf asks, having noticed Sam standing there.

Abby and Tabby run to Sam, latching on to each leg in a well-practiced move. "Don't go!" they both squeal at the same time. Sam has gotten used to their twin behaviors, which includes often saying the same thing.

"Don't be so silly," she laughs, prying them off her. "I'm just going to Cassy's. I'll be back by your bedtime and I'll help tuck you in!"

Satisfied, the two little girls run off. Racing to reach the ball they left behind, their dismay over their sister leaving is already forgotten. Shaking her head at their antics, Sam's mom then levels her gaze back on her older daughter.

"How about the homework? Math going okay?"

Sam hesitates. It's not like she had a chance to talk with her mom yet about the failed assignment. She just got it back this morning. She has to admit that she was hoping to redo it and get the new scores back before discussing it. However, now that her mom has asked, to *not* tell her would be as good as lying. But she's concerned that her mom might say she can't go to Covington Ranch.

"Sam?" Kathy presses.

"Well," Sam starts, looking down at her suddenly very interesting coat zipper. "I got all of my homework from today done, Mom. But I did horrible on my last assignment. I understand it now, though," she's quick to add, looking up. "Mr. Cooper explained what I did wrong and showed me how to fix it. He's letting me re-do it and I *almost* have it done. I promise to finish it when I get back."

"I think that you understand why I'd like you to complete it *before* you run off to do something else." Holding a hand up to stop Sam from moaning a complaint, Kathy continues. "But I know that you guys are working on a worthwhile fundraiser, so if you feel that you can get it finished tonight before bed, I won't say no. Just make sure you pull that grade up, Sam. I don't expect you to excel in all of your classes, but I *do* want you to try your hardest."

Relieved, but also feeling a little guilty, Sam nods once in agreement. "I will, Mom. Thanks. See you later!"

Running off before her mom can change her mind, Sam jogs outside. She's relieved that Hunter was in his room and wasn't there to hear their conversation. He's always looking for things to tease Sam about, and that would have given him enough material for weeks!

Jumping on her mountain bike, she cuts across the crunchy grass in the front yard of their small, tidy house. While it sits on a nice, three-acre lot, the house itself is rather modest. They might not have much money, but her parents have always taken pride in caring for their home.

Peddling up their tree-lined street, Sam passes Ally house and waves, even though she doesn't see anyone. The Parker's estate is a rather stark contrast to the Wolf's. The two-story Tudor-style house is full of expensive accents and furniture, but their yard is barely a quarter acre. While Ally prefers the warm, often noisy atmosphere of Sam's house, the large recreation room at Ally's is the perfect meeting spot for the group of friends, especially when their brothers join them.

Focusing back on the road, Sam feels a pang of loneliness. She and Ally do pretty much everything together, but it feels like as they grow older and take on more responsibilities, it's becoming harder to manage. Both Cassy and Ally will turn thirteen in less than two months. Teenagers. Her own birthday isn't until May, but it seems like she just had her twelfth!

Straining now against the incline, Sam concentrates on getting up the hill without stopping. It's a game the friends all play whenever making this journey. Ally *always* make it, but Sam and Cassy are sometimes forced to walk their bikes the final leg.

Grunting with satisfaction as she crests the top, Sam then leans back and coasts, letting her legs rest. She almost regrets wearing her warmer jacket. She worked up quite a sweat!

Letting go of the handlebars, Sam tilts her head up and closes her eyes briefly. Relishing the small thrill that stirs in her chest at the danger of riding blindly, she breathes in the crisp air, tinged with the familiar smell of pine.

Lisa Covington owns almost all of the woods on this hill and they're full of wonderful trails. Most of them were carved out of the dirt years ago, but there are also some new ones that the girls have worked hard to clear.

The sound of an approaching vehicle jars Sam out of her meditation. Jerking back to attention, she grabs at the handles and almost topples over before correcting the wobble she causes.

It turns out at that her reaction was unnecessary, as the car is still quite a ways ahead of her. If it had been moving at a normal speed it would have almost reached her, but instead it's crawling along, barely moving.

As the white, four-door sedan slowly draws nearer, Sam notices a large decal on the side of the driver's door, closest to her. It's the outline of an oval with the bold, black letters 'sTb' in the middle. Sam saw the same logo on Kendra Pierce's lab coat!

Both the driver and passenger have their windows rolled down in spite of the cold, and the two men are leaning out of the car, scanning the woods. It almost seems like they're looking for something. Or someone.

Sam stops her bike and watches them quietly as they drive past her. When the driver finally notices her, his startled expression is almost funny. But instead of saying hi, or perhaps letting her know what they're looking for so she can help, he yanks his head back inside the vehicle.

The brake lights flash on and the hair on the back of Sam's neck suddenly stands up, as if a charge of static electricity were nearby. Her solid instinct for danger has been proven many times this past year. She gets ready to ride away as fast she can, while at the same time fumbling for the phone in her jacket pocket.

The white reverse lights flash on briefly but then go dark, and the car abruptly speeds away, accelerating dangerously around the next curve in the road. A little shaken, Sam lets out her pent-up breath and rides in the opposite direction, glad that she's almost to the entrance of the ranch.

While the men in the car didn't actually do anything wrong or even *say* anything to her, Sam has no doubt that they were up to no good. She thinks back to Kendra Pierce's late work nights, dirty lab coat, and tear-streaked face.

Sam doesn't believe in coincidences.

6

CONNECTIONS

"I *definitely* like this one the best!" Hunter declares around a mouthful of shortbread.

Sam rolls her eyes at him and then goes back to mixing the ingredients into the large bowl in front of her. He said the same thing about the last five desserts he 'tested'. John and Hunter are both lounging at the center island in the large, country-style kitchen of the Covington Ranch. Cassy, Ally, Lisa Covington, and her Aunt Clara are all in various stages of preparation for a wide-range of cookies and cakes.

An apron suddenly flies across the room, hitting Hunter in the chest with a smacking sound. "All right guys," Clara states loudly with flour-encrusted hands on her hips. "If you want to continue eating, then you better get to baking."

While Hunter makes an attempt at dragging his feet, John is quick to jump into action. His cheeks burn hot under his mop of blonde hair, embarrassed at being reprimanded. Even though it isn't their fundraiser, he has a stronger sense of responsibility than his younger friend does. Standing around while other people work isn't something he normally does. Grabbing the other apron that Clara is holding out, John awkwardly ties it on while she turns back to grab the bowl she'd been occupied with.

"Here," Clara says, handing the chocolate chip cookie dough to John. "Shape these into one inch blobs and space them two inches apart on a cookie sheet. Make sure the oven is at three-hundred-and-fifty degrees before you put them in for ten minutes. Got it?"

Nodding, John smiles at her, happy to have an assignment. "Yes, ma'am."

Laughing now at Hunters dramatic display as he drags himself before Clara for his orders, Sam goes back to her own work. It's already Friday night and the bake sale is tomorrow morning. While it's only six o'clock and they have a lot done, they still have a long ways to go. It'll be a late night. Good thing they planned on making it a sleep-over, although they'll lose the boys at nine.

"What did Mrs. Spartan say today when you called?" Cassy asks Sam. Wiping at her cheek, she leaves a white streak behind, making her appear like a football player with the wrong color grease on her face.

"Rocky is still there," Sam answers while tossing a homemade caramel into her mouth. She has a feeling that she's going to be sick of sweets before the night is through.

"Have any more dogs shown up with the allergy symptoms?" Ally wants to know.

Shaking her head, Sam looks up at Ally. "No, but Mrs. Spartan, I mean Trish, said that she finds it odd no one has come looking for them. She thinks that both Rocky and the other dog are purebred and not more than a year or two old. I guess a papered miniature poodle can cost you more than five-hundred dollars. The one brought in Monday is a Bichon, which is just as expensive."

"I had a miniature poodle growing up," Aunt Clara says, joining the conversation. "Smartest dog I ever had!"

"I can tell that Rocky is smart," Sam agrees. "I've never had a dog stare at me without looking away like he does." Her eyes sting at the thought of the gentle dog sitting alone in his cage and she does her best to quickly change the subject. "Ally, did you get a chance to find out where Ms. Pierce works?"

Sam talked to Ally and Cassy about the strange car and the two men inside, but neither of them have a clue as to what the logo stands for. Between her extra homework and time put into the bake sale, she hasn't given it much more thought the past few days.

"I haven't seen her since Tuesday night," Ally answers. Pulling the oven door open, she removes the cupcakes that are done and puts in the cookies that her brother just finished preparing according to Clara's directions. "But I think you're right, Sam. Something weird is definitely going on with her job. Ms. Pierce has never asked me to watch Clara so many times in the same month. And she's been upset when she comes to pick her up. Even on the phone when she calls to ask me, I can tell that something is wrong. It seems like whatever it is that's keeping her there happens unexpectedly."

"Where does she work?" John asks, getting in on the intriguing conversation.

"I don't know," Ally says, wiping her hands on a towel. "I know she just finished college when Cora was born and that she majored in chemistry. She was excited about her new job, working at a lab, but when we exchanged information the first time that I babysat a couple of years ago, all she gave me and Mom was her cellphone number. I don't normally babysit during the week, because she's usually home from work before the daycare center closes and she picks Cora up herself. It's always been when Ms. Pierce goes out somewhere on the weekend, so *where* she worked never mattered."

"Well, how many labs can there be around here?" Hunter adds with his mouth again full of some sort of pastry.

"Are you going to actually make anything, or just eat it?" Lisa asks Hunter, pointing at the still-empty mixing bowl in front of him. Turning her focus onto Sam, her eyes narrow slightly. "Why do you need to know, Sam? Don't you think an adults issues with work are something you shouldn't get involved in?"

Sam blushes at the soft lecturing. She's been in trouble several times in just the last year for not minding her own business. In fact, if it weren't for her nosiness, Lisa herself would likely not own her home anymore, or even know that Cassy was her half-sister. Resisting the strong urge to point that out, Sam instead considers the older woman's statement. Not only is she Cassy's sister and her teacher, but she's also a friend and Sam respects her advice.

Is she right? Scrunching her forehead in concentration, Sam taps at her lip with the end of the mixing spoon. Maybe. "Do you think your mom could talk to her?" Sam finally asks Ally. "You know, just to make sure she doesn't need help with anything. She really seemed upset," she adds, turning back to Lisa.

Lisa nods her approval to Sam's suggestion. "Well then, perhaps Mrs. Parker can give her a shoulder to lean on. You know, as a single mom,

I'm sure that Kendra has a lot going on. It may very well have nothing to do with work."

"I guess ... " Sam says slowly, still tapping her lip. "But there was the work car the other day and the guys in it were acting really strange."

"What work car?" John questions, now also interested.

"Sam -- " Lisa cautions. She knows her young friend too well and her knack for finding mysteries.

Sam describes the encounter from the other day in detail, trying to capture the sense of danger that she had. Not fully succeeding, she's met with heavy scrutiny.

"So, because of some stupid car driving slowly and your over-active imagination, you think that Cora's mom is in trouble?" Hunter says with heavy sarcasm.

Having it put that way; Sam begins to question herself, too. Waving him off, she goes back to mixing. "You weren't there, so you just don't know what it was like, Hunter. It's not like I'm accusing them of anything, you guys. I just want to know what the name of the lab is!"

John pulls his cell phone out of his back

pocket. He's perched on a chair in front of the stove, watching his cookies bake, so he has a few spare minutes. "What did this logo look like?" he asks, looking up at Sam.

Relieved to have someone that wasn't over-reacting, Sam describes it to him in detail. "I already tried searching for the letters sTb," she explains. "I added lab and Oceanside to the search but still didn't get any hits."

Nodding his approval at her attempts, John taps at the screen for a few minutes. "Hmmm," he finally mumbles. "You're right. There isn't anything under the acronym or with labs, Oceanside, technology, or company. However," he adds, suddenly grinning, "when I combine all of them and add research, I got a name!"

Leaning forward eagerly, Sam momentarily forgets about the chocolate cake she's making. Everyone else in the room seems to have taken an interest, too.

"SynthTech Biolab," John announces. "They don't have a website or anything, which is why they're so hard to find. They're listed as a corporation though, with the company info. It sounds like they're a really small lab that makes bases and stuff for products ranging from makeup to blood tests."

Sam isn't sure exactly what that is, but it doesn't sound very exciting.

"Well, there ya go," Hunter says, spreading his arms wide. "No ultra-secret spy lab."

Glaring at her brother, Sam turns her attention back to John. "Where's it at?"

But John's expression has changed and he's now frowning down at his phone. The timer starts to beep and Ally removes the cookies for him.

"What's wrong?" Sam asks.

"Nothing," John replies. "It's just that my old Chemistry teacher is listed as the owner! He retired last year to take care of his wife, who's sick with cancer. Leave this one alone, Sam," he says as he puts his phone away with purpose. "Mr. Carpenter doesn't need any extra grief. He's a good man."

Even though John isn't scolding Sam in any way, and is only asking her to back off, she feels about two-feet tall. She looks up to him, and any kind of admonishment from him is a crushing blow. Determined not to upset John, or make

Lisa question her motives any further, Sam decides to follow his advice and let it go.

But sometimes, for Sam, that simply isn't possible.

7

A FURRY MYSTERY

The atmosphere is almost festive in the shelter. Ally, Cassy, and Sam are still celebrating the huge success of the bake sale from the day before. They raised more than enough to purchase the needed mattresses for the woman's shelter and even have some left over. That money will go back into the clubs account, to be used for the next event.

"What kind of fundraiser do you think we should do for the animal shelter?" Pauline asks. She's clearly impressed with her young friend's enthusiasm.

Sam rests her head on top of Rocky's, while mulling over the question. The poodle is happily curled up in her lap. She was so relieved to see him, that she almost cried. Even though she'd called only two days ago to check on him, she was convinced he'd be gone when she got there.

"It's still too cold out for a carwash," Cassy replies.

"Definitely!" Ally agrees, hugging herself against the imaginary cold.

They're all gathered in the grooming area, where Pauline is working on washing a large Great Dane. Cassy has a Terrier mix in the other sink and Ally is sitting on the floor next to Sam, waiting her turn. She has a tiny little Pomeranian, who's still shaking in spite of the warm blanket Ally's wrapped around it.

Rocky is already washed and dried and Sam knows that it's going to be hard to put him back in his kennel. However, ten other dogs also need baths and it's close to noon. After that, they have to clean all of their cages, take them on walks, and then spend some time with the cats. After working there for only two Sunday's, it's already obvious to Sam that the shelter desperately needs more employees. She's not convinced that their fundraiser will be able to do enough. They need long-term solutions.

"A dog show!" Sam suddenly shouts, the idea coming to her out of nowhere. Everyone looks expectantly at her and she blushes, fumbling to explain it. "I mean ... what if we ... You know, put on a local dog show? We could use the gym and set it up like those fancy shows you see on TV. Except that the dogs in it can be whatever breed and the kids can show them!" Sam likes her idea even more, as she thinks it through. "Pauline, you and Trish can be the judges and we'll give out ribbons to the winners."

"We can have an entry fee and also charge people to come watch it," Ally adds, smiling at Sam.

"Let's have cats in it, too!" Cassy laughs, tossing her sudsy hands up in the air.

"I love it!" Pauline gasps. "What an amazing idea. Trish is going to go crazy over this!"

Before they have a chance to discuss it further, the front door rings, announcing a visitor.

"Hello!" John shouts from out front.

Scrambling to her feet with a startled Rocky, Sam rushes out to find both Hunter and John waiting there. "What are you guys doing here?" she asks, surprised to see them.

"We wanted to come by and tell you guys the final numbers from the bake sale. Lisa finished adding it all up." John hands Sam a small spiral notebook containing the figures and she gulps in response.

Maybe, with some really good planning, the dog show **could** *make a difference!* Sam thinks, getting more excited. Looking up, she smiles at the boys.

"Is that the infamous Rocky?" Hunter asks, pointing at the poodle. He's been hearing about the dog non-stop for a week now.

Stepping towards her brother, Sam hands the dog out to him. Moving away from her, he raises his hands defensively. "I'm allergic!" he protests.

Shaking her head, Sam proceeds to place the dog in his arms. "Poodles don't shed, so a lot of people who have allergies can have them as pets. Plus, I just gave him a bath. Trish told me that the allergens are in their skin. So, it's really the dandruff that's stuck to the shedding hair that you're allergic to."

Hunter doesn't look convinced as he takes the dog, holding him awkwardly. Rocky gives him a quizzical look before licking him once on the nose, causing John to break out in loud laughter.

Not waiting to see what happens, Sam runs back to share the great news with her friends. When Hunter and John follower her a couple of minutes later, Sam smiles at how Hunter is now holding Rocky like a baby.

"Hey, guys, I'm Pauline. You have to be the notorious brothers, John and Hunter."

The boys introduce themselves and then Pauline offers to give them a tour, leaving the three younger girls to finish the grooming. When they return a short time later, Hunter and John are each leading a dog on a leash. Sam realizes that Rocky must be back in his kennel, and she does her best not to react.

"I've recruited them," Pauline explains, grinning. "They've graciously offered to help us walk the dogs today."

Sam and Hunter exchange a look and he gestures down at the white, fluffy Bichon, which is suffering from the same missing clumps of hair and red eyes as Rocky. "Pauline said that this guy is hyper-allergenic, too."

As they walk past Sam to head outside,

something about the comment causes Sam to pause, but she can't quite figure out why.

"Here," Pauline says, interrupting her thoughts. "Your next patient."

Sam takes the young black lab from her boss and immediately gets to work washing him. The next two hours are spent in a flurry of soap, fur, brushes, and dryers with little time to concentrate on anything else.

By three o'clock, they're working on the last batch of dogs and John and Hunter just left with the final two to walk the trail. Pauline is up front restocking the small assortment of pet supplies they keep on hand to sell. All that's left to do is to spend time petting and talking to the cats. Sam is already looking forward to the cat room, which will be super easy, compared to everything else.

Turning the loud dryer off, Sam lifts the dog she was drying and heads for the kennel room. On the way, she hears Pauline having a conversation with a man and woman up front.

Just as Sam slides the latch closed on the kennel, Pauline walks in smiling.

"The owners of the Bichon are here!" she says happily. "Just like the other dog, they claim that her skin and fur were perfect before she went missing a couple of weeks ago."

"Well, I'm sure glad that they found her!" Sam responds, but she looks worriedly at Rocky, who is watching her from his kennel. Will his owners come soon, too? Walking over to him as Pauline leaves with the Bichon, she opens his cage and kneels down. Reaching out to scratch behind both of his ears, she notes how the redness in his eyes is already nearly gone. New fur has started to grow back, filling in the few spots of bare skin he had. Glad to see that he's healing so fast, she plants a kiss on his head before going back to the other girls.

"Ready to see the cats?" Ally asks when Sam walks in. Placing an arm around her friend's shoulder, it's clear that she knows what Sam was doing in the other room.

Nodding silently, Sam allows herself to be led but peeks out front, as they walk past the opening. What she sees causes her to stop suddenly and her eyes widen in shock.

Standing in the open front door saying goodbye to Pauline, is the driver of the white car in the woods! Held clumsily in his arms is the little Bichon, and as they go out the door, it looks at Sam, shaking in fear.

8

GOOD INTENTIONS

"But you *can't* let him take the dog!"

Sam is holding onto Pauline's arm, pulling her back towards the front door of the shelter that just closed behind the suspicious man. The teen is looking at Sam skeptically.

"Sam, what in the world are you talking about?" Pauline gasps, shaking her arm loose. "They knew some distinguishing marks and the dog isn't chipped. How do you know it isn't theirs?"

Hesitating, Sam looks desperately out the large front window, where she can see the couple crossing the street. "It's hard to explain, but I don't think that man is really the owner. He was driving a company car the other day for this lab and acting really strange."

Squinting now at Sam, her nose scrunched up, Pauline is clearly not getting it. "Explain 'strange'."

"Well," Sam shuffles her feet, looking to Ally for some help. When Ally shrugs, she takes a breath and rushes to tell the story. "They were driving really slow. Oh, there was another guy in the car. Anyway, they were driving really slow with their windows down and when they saw me on my bike, they stopped. After sitting there for a minute, they started to back up like they were going to move towards me, but then sped off really fast!" Gulping in another breath, Sam looks hopefully at Pauline.

"So, you mean that they were acting like someone who might have been out looking for a lost dog? And that perhaps when they saw a gal on a bike, they considered asking you if perhaps *you* had seen the dog?" Pauline has crossed her arms, and is watching Sam, waiting for an answer.

Her face growing hot, Sam's spirits fall. She can no longer see the man outside. "There's more than that," Sam attempts one last time. "The mom of a little girl we babysit works at the same lab and has been acting really strange lately. Please," Sam begs, "can't you just ask the man some more questions? I mean, did the dog even respond to the name he called it? It looked scared when they were leaving."

Her expression changing from confusion to anger, Pauline's back goes rigid. "Sam, I've been doing this job a little longer than you have. Do you really think I'd let a dog go with someone that I thought was lying?"

Horrified at having insulted her new friend, Sam forgets about the dog for the moment. "Oh! I didn't mean - "

"Besides," Pauline continues, cutting Sam off. "He made a sizable donation to the shelter for taking care of the dog." Waving a check in the air, Pauline walks around to the cash register to place it inside, clearly dismissing Sam's concerns. "I know that it's hard sometimes to let the animals go, Sam. Especially if you get attached to them ... or name them."

Looking down at the floor, Sam feels the heat growing in her face and spreading to the top of her head. Ally, Cassy, John, and Hunter are all in the room with front-row seats to her scolding.

"Pauline, the dog really *did* look scared," Ally adds quietly, stepping up to place a supportive hand on Sam's elbow. "Wouldn't it normally be happy to see its owner?

"He called her 'Baby' and she perked up when he spoke to her, like she recognized him, okay?" Pauline says to Ally, slapping her hands on the counter. "Baby has had a rough couple of weeks, so who can blame her for not acting what you consider 'normal' for a dog. Look," she continues, smoothing down some stray hairs from her ponytail. "Working at a shelter is tough and can be very emotional, but you have to learn to control that or it isn't going to be a job you can do."

Sam looks up sharply at Pauline, to find the older girl staring hard at her. It's difficult to tell if she's mad at Sam, or concerned. Maybe a little of both. "I'm sorry, Pauline," Sam says sincerely. "I didn't mean to be so … pushy. I'm just worried about the dog."

Her face softening slightly, Pauline comes out from behind the counter and then leans back against it. "I know you *mean* well, Sam. But aside from our main goal of helping animals, this is also a business. We have to act professionally at all times, or else it might damage our reputation. We're walking a thin-line here as it is and we can't afford to lose any more donors. Mr. Clancy, Baby's owner, indicated that he might be interested in contributing more to the shelter. Do you think that would still happen if I'd let you run after him and accuse him of lying about that being his dog?" Shaking her head, Pauline pushes away from the counter. "Just go finish up with the cats, okay? It's been a long day and I still have to clean the grooming room."

Pauline leaves the room without another word and Sam looks back at the rest of the group. John puts a finger up to his lips and then motions for them all to start moving. Sam leads the way to the cat chamber, opting to go the roundabout way from behind the register, to avoid walking through the grooming area.

After selecting Yoda, the biggest, fluffiest cat she's ever encountered, Sam plops down on one of the many beanbags scattered on the floor. Ally, Cassy, and John all follow suit, but Hunter remains in the doorway.

"The antihistamine I took earlier might be keeping me alive while in this building," he explains, wiping at his nose. "But I'm pretty sure that if I even *think* about stepping in this room, I'll probably die."

Feeling bad for her brother, Sam realizes that he must still be suffering, even with the medicine. He normally has a hard time just being in someone's house if they have a dog or cat.

"And good going, Sherlock," he continues, leaning back against the doorframe with his arms crossed over his chest. "You might be the first in our family to get fired from a *volunteer* job."

Her concern rapidly evaporating, Sam glares at Hunter, trying to think up something equally hurtful to say.

"Sam might actually be right," John says before anyone else can respond.

Startled, Sam looks at John, the smart retort to her brother dying on her lips. Of all the people here, she figured John would be the most upset with her, given what he said about the lab the other night. "I am?" she says, her voice a little muffled as Yoda begins rubbing his voluptuous head against her face.

"Did anyone else see how much that check was for?" John asks, looking at each of them in turn. When no one says yes, he continues. "Well, I was walking by when Mr. Clancy was writing it and it was five-thousand dollars!"

"That's crazy!" Ally gasps, her eyes wide.

"That dog couldn't have been worth more than a thousand," Cassy adds.

"No wonder Pauline was willing to overlook a couple of things," Sam says, thinking about what it might mean. "That's a whole lot of money to the shelter."

"But why?" Ally asks. "Why would someone be willing to pay so much for a dog that isn't even theirs? And what does the lab have to do with it?"

"Maybe it *was* his dog," Hunter suggests. "Maybe the guy's just rich and wants to help out the shelter that saved his dog and he happens to work at the lab?"

Looking intently at her brother, Sam considers all of the options. Coming to a decision, her mouth sets in a determined line. "There's only one way to find out."

9

THE NOSE KNOWS

"Let me see it." Ally is holding a hand out to Sam, who's seated next to her on the overstuffed couch in Ally's rec room.

Sam reluctantly passes the three-page math test to her and then closes her eyes, waiting for the anticipated reaction. The test on Monday was totally unexpected and while she's finally doing better with her homework, she still got a C- on the exam.

"Well, I guess it could have been worse," Ally sighs. "Don't you normally have your weekly quiz on Thursday's?" When Sam nods, Ally hands the test back to her. "Then you better figure out why you missed those. You've got until tomorrow."

Leaning back into the deep cushion, Sam drapes the paper marked up with red ink across her face. "Why can't we be in the same class?" She says, her voice muffled by the test.

"You're funny, Sam!" Giggling, Cora throws a stuffed rabbit at Sam's midriff, startling her so that the math paper flutters to the floor. "What's this?" the little girl asks, picking it up.

"*This* is what happens to you when you get older, Cora," Sam explains, taking the papers and waving them in the air. "Enjoy kindergarten while you can, kid. It's all downhill from there."

Laughing again, Cora retrieves the rabbit and goes back to playing with it. In her other hand, she has a Barbie doll dressed like a cowboy. Setting the doll on the rabbits back, she proceeds to make it hop from one piece of furniture to the other, making whooping sounds as she goes.

Shaking her head at the little girl's antics, Sam takes out a calculator and gets to work. She has to go home soon and she might need Ally's help with some of the problems.

Her plans for the night are already ruined. When she came over after dinner, she was hoping to talk with John about how they can get some information on the lab. But he isn't even home. However, when she discovered that Cora was here, she decided to try to talk to Ms. Pierce, instead.

Sam is frustrated with the lack of any real plan yet. She wanted to find out where the lab was and simply drive up there and snoop around, but John flat out refused. He insisted that she give him the week to look into his old teacher, Mr. Carpenter.

Distracted again, Sam tries to focus on the paper in front of her, but Cora is now tugging at her leg.

"I gotta go to the bathroom."

"You know where it is, Cora," Ally says, saving Sam. "Do you need help?"

"Nah," the little girl shakes her head. "I use the bathroom all by myself when I go to Kindy-garten."

Sam smiles as the little girl struts down the hall, quite proud of herself. It won't be long before her sisters are that big. She's looking forward to the time when they're no longer in pull-ups.

A knock at the front door startles both girls,

and Ally's the first one to react. "It's got to be Ms. Pierce," she breathes, looking up at the clock. "She promised to be here before seven-thirty this time."

A minute later, Cora's mom joins them in the rec room to wait for her daughter, who still hasn't returned from the bathroom.

"Should we check on her?" Ally questions.

"Give her a couple of more minutes," Kendra says. "She's going through a phase right now where she sings a song twice while washing her hands. Cora saw it on a TV show last week and has been doing it ever since. It's actually a good habit, but I think she forgets the song, or how many times she's sung it, and ends up washing them for much longer than she needs to."

Laughing, Ally starts gathering up the toys that Cora brought with her. "She was really good tonight," she tells the older woman. "No tantrums."

"That's a relief," Kendra replies. "I don't plan on having many more of these late nights. It's too hard on her and I already don't spend enough time with Cora."

While Ally was moving about the room, Sam was carefully studying Kendra Pierce. While she isn't wearing a white lab coat this time, her face is once again red and puffy. She also keeps wiping at her nose.

"Are you okay, Ms. Pierce?" Sam finally asks, unable to keep silent any longer. "Are you sick?"

Looking startled, Kendra stops wiping her nose and turns slowly to face Sam. Staring at her for a moment, she squints slightly before shaking her head. "No, Sam. I'm fine. It's just allergies. I'm afraid that Cora inherited it from me. I'm allergic to just about everything, and sometimes one of the products we work with at the lab will cause me to have a reaction."

Seeing her opening, Sam pounces on it. "It must be a really interesting job! What kind of work do you do there?"

Chucking, Kendra stuffs her hands in her coat pockets. "Trust me, endlessly creating bases and other generic material for products is *not* exciting." Her eyes flick nervously from Sam's face to Ally's, and then to the hallway. "Maybe I *should* go get Cora now," she states a bit nervously.

"Do you know Mr. Carpenter?" Ally presses, before she leaves the room.

Pausing, Kendra slowly turns back. Her expression is neutral. "Of course I know him, he owns the company. But I hardly ever see the poor man. He spends most of his time at home, with his sick wife. Mr. Clancy pretty much runs the lab now."

Sam and Ally share a startled look, as Kendra disappears down the hall. It has to be the same Mr. Clancy that took the dog from the shelter! Voices approaching the room prevent Sam from asking Ally what she thinks it might all mean.

"I was talking with Lisa Covington yesterday and she had a wonderful idea!" Ally's mom is saying.

The two women reappear with Cora between them, who is still drying her hands on a towel she brought with her from the bathroom.

"Covington," Kendra repeats thoughtfully. "Is that the old horse ranch up on the hill?"

"Yes!" Elizabeth confirms, glancing at Ally. "Ally and Sam have become good friends with Lisa's younger sister, Cassy. The Covington ranch has sat empty for years, but Lisa has been busy renovating it and has plans to open a riding school this summer. She's got several horses now and is looking for some young riders to help her test out a riding schedule."

"I don't understand," Kendra replies. "She wants *Cora* to come up there and ride a horse? Isn't she a little small for that?"

"Lisa said that five is the youngest she'd take, but that Cora should be okay. Lisa would be leading the horse, of course, and then you or someone else would walk beside her. I just thought that it might make for a fun day for Cora and it would be totally free."

"Cora has horrible allergies to cats and dogs," Kendra states, obviously doubtful.

"Has she ever been near a horse?" Sam asks. "My brother Hunter has allergies too, but he's fine with horses."

"Part of it has to do with how well the horses are groomed and what they use in their stalls," Ally adds. "Lisa takes really good care of them and only uses the best grains and alfalfa. No dusty hay or anything."

"Well," Kendra hesitates. "I suppose we could give it a try. It would be nice to take Cora somewhere fun and spend a day together." Warming to the idea, she kneels down in front of her daughter. "What do you think? Want to go ride a horse this weekend?"

Bouncing up and down, Cora squeals with delight. "I wanna go ride a horse *now!*"

Realizing her mistake, Kendra moans. "Uh-oh." Taking Cora's hand, they head for the front door. "It's too late now, pumpkin. All the horses are already in bed."

"Horses sleep?"

Listening to the ongoing conversation as the two leave the house, Sam starts laughing. "Oh my gosh, I wonder if she falls asleep talking?"

"Thanks, Mom," Ally says, giving her mom a hug.

"I should have reached out to her a long time ago." Elizabeth looks down at her daughter. "Maybe I can go, too? I finally have a weekend off. I haven't been on a horse in forever!"

The conversation is interrupted by John and Hunter entering the room. Sam is happy to see them. Well, John anyways. She never knows what kind of mood her brother will be in.

"I'll go warm you guys up some dinner," Mrs.

Parker offers before heading to the kitchen.

"Mr. Clancy is running the lab!" Sam blurts, before anyone else has a chance to say anything.

Nodding, John plops down on the couch. "That would make sense. I asked around and I guess that Mr. Carpenter started the company years ago, as a plan for retirement, but he was forced to leave his teaching career early after his wife got sick. I'll bet Mr. Clancy has been in charge of things from the beginning."

"You don't really believe all this stuff about the dogs somehow being tied up in the lab?" Hunter says, waving his arms around.

"Why not?" Sam counters. "Animals are used for testing all the time, Hunter. The dogs that came into the shelter all have the same allergic conditions. There's something else."

All eyes turn on Sam, and Ally tilts her head questioningly at her friend's hesitation. Sam is looking down at her feet, while twisting her hands together nervously in front of her. "What is it, Sam?" she pushes. "Out with it!"

"Both Cora and her mom are allergic to dogs and when Ms. Pierce showed up with her dirty lab coat still on, Cora had an asthma attack. That was a few days before the dogs started showing up at the shelter."

"And Ms. Pierce said that *she's* been suffering from allergies, too, when you asked her about her symptoms!" Ally exclaims, looking at Sam.

"You geniuses are forgetting something," Hunter says smugly. "Rocky and those other dogs you told me about all have something in common. They're all what you guys call hyper-allergenic. So that blows your theory, if you think they came from the lab and caused the allergies."

Dejected, Sam hates to admit that her brother is right. "Wait a minute!" she says distractedly, getting up and pacing the room. "What are the odds that all of the dog breeds showing up with allergy symptoms are all types of breeds that don't shed? We're missing something here!"

"I might have a way to get inside and find out."

Everyone looks at John, waiting for him to continue.

"I have an assignment coming up that's part of my civics class. I just found out today that I have to choose a local business to write about." Looking pointedly at Sam, John grins. "I think I should pick SynthTech Biolab."

10

UNDERCOVER

The fluorescent lights stutter overhead, casting the room into a flickering array of shadows. Sam picks nervously at the corner of the spiral notebook on the table in front of her as she looks around the room. A soft kick at her foot, delivered by John sitting next to her, makes her aware that she's tapping it nervously against the floor. Stopping the motion, she swallows hard and tries to sit up straighter.

They're seated at a nice mahogany table in what was called the 'meeting' room by the receptionist. There are six padded office chairs around it, four of which are empty. John occupies the one to Sam's left, and they both face the only door to the room, which has remained closed now for nearly ten minutes.

John and Hunter picked the three girls up from school and they sat in the parking lot for nearly fifteen minutes, debating who would go inside with John. Since it's Friday, they have no idea what kind of hours the lab will keep. John wanted to get there as soon as possible. They finally decided that since Sam could identify both of the men in the car, as well as Kendra and the two dogs, that she should go with him.

She was excited by the prospect, up until the moment they got to the front reception desk and John gave his school paper research story. Sam's stomach sank somewhere near her knees and has remained there ever since. She keeps trying to swallow around the lump rising in her throat and is now making a dry coughing sound every few minutes. Reaching out, she pours herself a glass of water from the pitcher that's sitting in the middle of the table.

Looking sideways at her, John eyes her skeptically with his frosty blue eyes. "I thought you were into this kind of thing," he jests. "If you want to back out, I can say you had to go home or something."

Humiliation forces her stomach to settle, and Sam hardens her resolve. She's never backed down from a mystery. Because she's emotionally tied up with Rocky's involvement, the possible consequences are weighing heavy on her. Shaking her head, she meets John's gaze and holds it. "I'm fine," she offers, doing her best to smile. "I just don't like waiting."

Not convinced, John shifts in the chair to face her. But the door suddenly opens, causing him to turn back the other way before he can push the issue.

Relieved, Sam watches thoughtfully as Mr. Clancy enters the room. He looks to be in his thirties, with short brown hair and dark, piercing eyes. Her stomach threatens to revolt again, but she wraps her hands around the glass of water and then takes a long drink. They'd been hoping that someone other than the director would speak with them, since he might recognize John from the shelter or Sam from the woods. Slowing her breathing at the same time, Sam does her best to appear relaxed.

"So," the confident man says loudly, taking a

seat across from them. "I hear that you have an interest in our little lab?" If he *does* recognize them, he's doing a good job of hiding it.

"Yes, sir," John replies evenly. "I'm writing a paper for my civics class, and we're required to research a local business. Since I'm thinking of majoring in chemistry, I thought SynthTech Biolab would be a great place to write about."

Sam didn't know that John has such an interest in chemistry and she hopes that he isn't lying. It would be a small fib, but that isn't at all like him. Looking at John briefly, she notes how calm he appears and envies him slightly. He's a natural at this.

"And who's your helper?"

Startled, Sam looks at Mr. Clancy, realizing he's talking about her.

"She's a friend of mine," John says smoothly, delivering the excuse they'd come up with. "I'm giving her a ride home, so I dragged her along with me and I'm making her take notes."

Chuckling, Mr. Clancy appears to accept the explanation without question. "Smart boy," he says. "Never miss an opportunity for free help." Slapping the top of the glossy table, he stands abruptly. "Well, the thing with a lab is that it's much easier to show you what we do, rather than tell you. Follow me."

Taking Sam's elbow, John pulls her after him as they follow Mr. Clancy from the room and out into the hall. Exchanging a look, John gestures at the notebook she's clasping, reminding her to write stuff down. He's already scribbled several things on his own notepad, although she has no idea what it could be.

"Mr. Carpenter developed this company over ten years ago, and brought me on to head things up." Mr. Clancy pauses to look back at them while holding open another door. "You might know him, John. He used to teach at your school and I think he was an assistant football coach as well. I'm guessing a boy your size probably plays."

"He coached me for two years," John confirms while walking through the doorway. "And I took his chemistry class last year. It was tough when he had to leave."

Sam is right behind him, and discovers they've entered a large room full of rows of tables with various types of machinery. John and Mr.

Clancy continue their conversation as they walk and Sam remembers to write some of the most pertinent information down. Between all the talk about the business, and Mr. Clancy pointing at things and describing how they work, Sam is quickly lost. She has no interest in the boring details, or how one machine spins and another analyzes. John, on the other hand, seems fascinated.

After more than half-an-hour, they finally walk down a couple of different corridors, and eventually pass some bathrooms. It's what Sam's been waiting for. As soon as they enter the next room, she speaks up.

"Mr. Clancy, would it be okay if I use the bathroom? I think we just passed some back there," she adds, pointing back the way they came.

"Absolutely," he says. "We'll probably still be here. I just know John's going to want to see the new centrifuge Craig got for us last week."

Nodding as if she knows what a centrifuge is, Sam backs out of the room. Spinning on her heel, she begins looking at the other doors in the hall that they walked past. She'd seen very few other employees during the tour. In fact, most of the rooms were empty, except for the first lab area where there were three other men. They were all wearing the same lab coats and goggles and appeared to be in the middle of various experiments.

It's a large, maze-like building with oversized work areas connected by numerous hallways. It would be easy to get lost. Sam passes a door with a 'closet' sign on it before continuing on to the bathrooms. Feeling a bit guilty, she shuffles by, and then stops at the next corridor. It's one of only a few that Mr. Clancy didn't take them down. Peering around the corner, she's relieved to see that the way is clear. Hurrying along, her footsteps seem extra loud as they echo off the walls and she tries to walk more lightly.

There's only one door midway down, which indicates to Sam that the room beyond must be a big one. Stopping in front of it, she sees right away that it's different from the others. *Everything* has a sign on it. From the closet, to the bathroom, to the various labs. This one, however, is blank.

Reaching out, Sam tentatively tries the

doorknob. It doesn't turn under her hand. Frustrated, she takes a step back and crosses her arms. *How am I supposed to find anything if the doors are locked?* She wonders, looking up and down the long hallway. Time is slipping away and Mr. Clancy is going to wonder what happened to her.

Just as Sam starts to walk away, the door suddenly jerks open unexpectedly. Turning back with a startled gasp, Sam finds herself face-to-face with Kendra Pierce!

Freezing, Kendra holds a clipboard to her chest and then nervously looks back into the room she just came from. The door is slowly swinging shut, but before the gap is closed, Sam hears the distinct sound of a dog barking!

11

PAWFULLY SUSPICIOUS

"Why do I feel like *we* did something wrong?" Ally asks, pacing back and forth in front of the large TV in the rec room.

They drove straight to Ally and John's house after leaving the lab. Their parents aren't back from work yet, and Sam already texted her mom that they'd be going there. She likely expects Sam to spend the night, since it *is* Friday.

"Well, maybe it's because John took up that guys time for a fake tour and Sam, as usual, snuck off and nosed around in other people's business," Hunter sneers. Cramming his hand noisily into a bag of potato chips, his face is hard to read. He may or may not be serious.

"Hey, man, I really do have an assignment. That place is pretty cool and it's going to make a good paper." John is uncharacteristically defensive with his friend, and the tension in the room is now obvious.

"Nobody did anything wrong," Cassy intervenes, hating to see her two friends at odds. "And Ms. Pierce wasn't mad or anything. Right, Sam?"

Nodding, Sam tosses her notebook on the table. "Like I said before, she was just really nervous. And surprised. When I told her I was there with John for a class assignment she relaxed, but I don't think she totally bought the explanation. I'm going to have to talk to her," she adds, reluctantly coming to the realization.

Running her hands through her shoulder-length hair, Sam looks at her friends and then finally her brother. "I might have to agree with you this time, Hunter. At least partway. I *was* nosing around and doing exactly what Lisa told me I shouldn't do. Now, Ms. Pierce is probably even more upset than she was before. Because I'm positive now, more than ever, that she's caught up in something. You should have seen the guilt on her face! And there were definitely dogs in that room."

"Maybe we should ask Lisa or my mom to talk to her instead?" Ally suggests. "Damage control now might be easier than later."

"No," Sam says without even thinking about it. "Trying to explain all of this and dragging them into it will probably just get us into trouble, and then nothing will be done about the dogs!" Thinking about Rocky being taken back to that locked room strengthens Sam's conviction. "We *have* to figure out how to get those dogs out of there!"

Spinning, Sam looks pleadingly at John, who's been quiet since his exchange with Hunter. He's leaning against the computer desk with a guarded expression on his handsome features.

"Just because you don't like the fact that they have dogs there, doesn't mean that they're doing anything wrong," he finally says. Putting up a hand to stop Sam's retort, he then turns and powers up the computer. "I think you might be getting ahead of yourself, Sam," he continues while tapping at some keys. "The last thing we want to do is run around accusing a legitimate business of doing something illegal, when we really have no idea *what's* going on."

Sam briefly wonders if having John go in for the tour might be backfiring. He really seemed taken by the whole experience, and now he's defending them! Looking desperately at Ally, she widens her eyes and raises her eyebrows questioningly.

"I get what he's saying," Ally says quietly to her friend. She knows how attached Sam has become to Rocky, but John is right. "Think about it, Sam. We might have already blown our friendship with Ms. Pierce. Trish has called us all in for a special meeting tomorrow, where you're likely to get in trouble for being suspicious of that guy last weekend, and this is John's old teachers business! We need to be more careful about not doing anything that's possibly hurtful to other people. But," she adds, looking now at her brother. "You know that Sam is usually right about this kind of stuff, and I think that we all agree that something is fishy."

"So let's start with what might be going on," Hunter joins in. Coming to stand behind John, he looks at what he's doing on the computer. Nodding in approval, he points at one of the site hits on the screen. "Try that one." Facing Ally, he tips his head slightly to look down at her. "You do know that dogs are used for research, right?"

"Except that SynthTech Biolab isn't a research lab. Right, John?" Ally counters.

"Right," he answers. "Mr. Clancy confirmed yesterday what I already read about the company. All they create are bases and other mundane ingredients for products for other labs that do the research stuff."

"What if Mr. Carpenter had a special project?" Sam taps at her chin, thinking aloud. "What if he's trying to come up with some sort of cure for his wife's cancer?"

"Oh!" Cassy gasps, coming to stand with the rest of them. "That would make sense, but it seems like a stretch. I mean, huge corporations all over the world are throwing tons of money at that. Isn't this a pretty small place in comparison?"

"Yeah," John replies. "And according to this business report," he says, pointing at the monitor, "nobody at SynthTech Bioloab is getting rich. It's impressive for a company here in Oceanside, but we're talking about a set-up that's worth hundreds of thousands, not tens of millions, which is what you'd need for that kind of program."

"So why the dogs?" Sam repeats the question. The five friends all look at each other solemnly.

"They're all breeds that don't shed," Ally states. "They all showed up at the shelter with severe allergy symptoms the week after Ms. Pierce started acting strange. Then, she and Cora both have allergic reactions to whatever was on her lab coat. Maybe it's the obvious," Ally suggests, directing her statement at Sam. "Maybe the lab *is* doing research now, but it's not for anything monumental like a cancer cure, but rather a skin product for allergies or something."

"That makes the most sense," Hunter replies, slapping his hands together. "Who's hungry? Isn't it dinner time, or snack time or something?"

Pushing at Hunter playfully, Cassy directs him towards the kitchen. "Is it okay if we graze?" she asks Ally, relieved to have things back to normal.

Waving them off, she laughs at her friends. "Mom texted me a little while ago that she'll be late, so we can go ahead and order some pizza. I'll call in a few minutes."

Sam waits for Hunter's whoops of joy to die down before voicing her opinion. "I think you might be right," she tells Ally, stuffing her hands in the back pockets of her jeans. "But I'm not convinced that it's legit. Why would Ms. Pierce act so strange about it, and why would Mr. Clancy put on the act for the shelter, if it's all legal?"

"There are a lot of groups that protest animal testing," John states. "I'm sure that even if they had all the proper permits and stuff, they'd still want to keep it quiet to avoid any bad publicity."

"So how do we find out?" Ally wonders. "I wouldn't know where to begin. Who's even in charge of that kind of stuff? It's not like the police would even do anything about it. Isn't it a state thing?"

"I'll bet Trish would know!" Sam exclaims, smiling. "We can ask her about it when we see her tomorrow, and then I can talk to Ms. Pierce about it on Sunday."

"She's bringing Cora over at nine on Sunday morning," Cassy says as she walks back into the room. She's already eaten half of the apple in her hand.

"Yeah, that reminds me," Ally replies. "Cassy and I need to ask Trish tomorrow if we can take half the day off Sunday. I want to spend it with my mom at Covington Ranch."

Smiling at Ally, Sam is happy for her friend. It isn't that often that she gets to spend a day with her mom. It reminds Sam how lucky she is, that her own mom chose to quit working as a teacher to stay home with the twins.

"I'm sure she'll be okay with it," Sam assures Ally and Cassy. "I'm going to run home for a little bit," she tells them all. "I want to make sure mom doesn't need help with the twins for dinner, and I can grab my stuff for tonight. I'll be back before the pizza gets here!"

Giving Ally and Cassy a quick hug, Sam scoots from the room. She has another, ulterior motive to speaking to her mom alone. Now, more than ever, she feels an urgency to make sure Rocky is spared any more harm. The shelter has a mandatory two-week hold for found dogs, before they'll put them up for adoption. If he *did* escape the lab, they're probably waiting to claim him to throw off any suspicion. But even if he really is a stray, he'll be available for adoption starting this weekend.

Doing her best to compose herself before entering the house, Sam thinks about all the brilliant arguments she came up with to convince her mom to let her bring Rocky home.

12

A WIDENING WEB

Rocky snatches the ball up in his mouth before prancing over to where Sam is sitting with her back up against his kennel. Dropping it, he tilts his head slightly to give her a quizzical look and then whimpers.

"It's okay," Sam whispers before wiping at a stray tear. "I'm just sad that you can't come live with me."

Sam came early to the meeting by herself, so that she'd have time to play with her friend. She feels as if she's failed him, by not being able to make her mom understand how perfect he is. Scratching at the sweet spot behind his ears, Sam then picks up the ball and tosses it again.

As he runs down the length of the kennel room, Sam wonders if she'll even get to work here anymore. The only reason she waited so long to talk to her mom was that she'd doubted that Sam could handle it in the first place. She wasn't going to let Sam volunteer at first, because she was afraid she'd get too attached to the animals. Of course, that's exactly what her mom said last night. That she was right and that Sam would want to bring home a dog a week, if she said yes.

"But she's wrong, Rocky," Sam says to the dog. "You're special. There'll never be another dog like you."

As another round of fresh tears blurs her vision, a comforting hand warms Sam's shoulder. She doesn't need to look up to know that it's Ally.

"Your mom said no?" she asks gently.

Nodding silently, Sam covers her face with her hands. She doesn't cry very often and she hates doing it in front of other people. Even Ally.

"That's why you were so quiet when you came back last night," Ally says, sitting down next to her friend. She knows how much Rocky means to Sam and is already trying to think up a way to turn things around. "Maybe you could arrange to have him come over for a day? I'm sure Trish would be okay with it. Then, your mom could see how great he is and that Hunter really isn't allergic to him."

"I don't think Mom would go for it," Sam sighs, working hard to compose herself. "You know how stubborn she is once she decides on something. Dad's calling tomorrow night, though," she adds. Turning to Ally, the beginning of a smile tugs at her lips. "I can ask him to talk to Mom. He's a softy for animals. If he suggests the visit, she could go for it. It's a good idea, Ally. Thanks."

Hugging her friend tightly, Ally then stands and offers a hand to Sam. "Cassy's out front and Trish seems eager to talk to us. We'd better get out there."

Taking Ally's hand, Sam struggles to her feet and then shakes out her stiff legs. She's been sitting here on the floor for nearly twenty minutes. Sniffing, she lifts up the bottom of her sweatshirt and uses it to wipe her face. "Can you tell I was crying?" she asks Ally.

Hesitating, Ally carefully choses her words. "Only a little. No one is going to say anything, Sam."

"Except I'll look like even more of a sap to Trish." Calling to Rocky, the two of them walk out together.

Fifteen minutes later, Sam is staring down at her hands in her lap. Trish spent the last ten minutes saying pretty much all the same stuff her mom lectured her on last night.

The four of them are all in Trish's small office. There were only two chairs facing her desk, so Sam chose to sit on the floor with Rocky. She knew that Trish was likely upset with her, so being out of her direct line of sight seemed a good idea.

Upset is probably too strong of a word. More like disappointed, which is even worse in some ways. Sam forces herself to look up and meet the older woman's gaze. "I'm sorry, Trish," she says sincerely. "I didn't mean to question Pauline's judgement," she adds, repeating the director's choice of words. "And I know it looks like I was suspicious of Mr. Clancy because I'm too attached to the dogs, but that really isn't why."

"She's right," Cassy says, eager to support her friend. "There's something strange about the lab that guy works at."

They'd agreed last night that they would try to get some information from Trish about the laws and animal testing, but without making any accusations. Sam's stomach tightens slightly at Cassy's comment. She appreciates her standing up for her, but they have to be careful not to say too much.

"It's okay, Cassy," Sam quickly says. "Trish is right. I shouldn't have jumped to conclusions like that. I promise that it won't happen again."

Studying Sam for a minute, Trish is clearly debating how to proceed. "Ally and Cassy, I know you would like to take part of tomorrow off," she says, turning her attention to the other two girls. "Why don't you all take the whole day? Things have been slower this past week, and I need to spend some time with Pauline, anyways."

While it seems like a perfectly reasonable suggestion, Sam can't help but feel like it's a punishment. Reaching out to pet Rocky's back, she wonders briefly if she can still stop by to see him.

"Then, why don't you come by after school next Friday to meet with me. We can discuss if this is a good fit for you. If you'd like to continue volunteering we'll figure out a more permanent schedule."

Sam wishes now that she could see Ally and Cassy's expressions, instead of staring at their backs. She isn't sure how to take Trish's suggestion. It feels like a mix of both negative and positive. Maybe she means that it'll be good fit for some of them, but not all? Feeling more dejected, Sam debates whether or not to even ask Trish the questions they'd come up with last night. It could very well seal her fate.

Rocky chooses this moment to look up at her. Caught by those warm, chocolate-brown eyes, Sam thinks of the barking she heard in the lab and knows she has to press forward. They have to do all they can to rescue those dogs, if they aren't there legally.

Trish is already starting to stand behind her desk, clearly ready to dismiss them. Sam jumps to her feet and rushes to ask the first question on the list they made.

"Trish, we were wondering what exactly is

involved in using dogs for tests and stuff."

Pausing, Trish turns slowly towards Sam, her eyes narrowed. "What do you mean?"

It's instantly clear that this isn't going to go well, but Sam is committed now and so she pushes on. "Well, if a University or someone wanted to use animals for tests, aren't there laws and permits, and stuff that they'd have to get? Who makes sure that they're following the law?"

Crossing her arms, the older woman is ominously quiet. Slowly, she sits back down at her desk. "The main law is called the AWA, or Animal Welfare Act. There have been several amendments to it over the years, to tighten up the regulations, but it's very extensive. It's enforced by the federal government. The USDA, to be precise. The penalties for violating the laws are steep and taken very seriously. It's rare to find an organization stepping outside the protocols. There's a lot involved in even getting permits to use rats and mice, let alone canines or felines."

Ally turns slightly so that she can see Sam, and the two of them exchange a wary look. It's clear by her tone of voice, that Trish isn't happy about the question.

"Look, you guys," Trish continues, leaning back in her chair. Her typically untidy bun is messier than normal, and her hazel eyes are guarded. "I've been actively involved in animal rights before and believe me, if there was anyone locally applying for the use of lab animals, I'd know about it. I still have connections. I realize you have a habit of getting *involved* in things, Sam." Leaning forward now, Trish points a harsh finger at her. "But when it comes to this shelter, I don't expect my employees to take it upon themselves to nose around my customers business. Mr. Clancy is now a big contributor. One of our largest, to be precise, and I -- *we*, can't afford to have anyone making ridiculous statements about what he may or may not be doing. Am I making myself clear?"

Swallowing hard, Sam tries to control her rush of emotions. They made a big mistake. She should have known better than to think they could involve Trish without her immediately putting it all together. But then … Sam instantly goes from feeling shame to a growing anger. If it's so obvious, why isn't Trish the one asking the questions? Could it be that the director has been bought off? That she's willing to turn a blind eye for a few thousand dollars? Or maybe it's even something worse. The lab is getting its animals from somewhere. What better way to operate secretly, than to have an 'in' at a local shelter?

Her face burning now, Sam faces Trish with a stony resolution. "Yes, Mrs. Spartan, you're being perfectly clear."

13

QUESTIONS

The small mare tosses her head and snorts, causing another round of contagious laughter from her rider. Cora is sitting astride the horse like a pro, surprising her mom. So far, there aren't any signs of an allergic reaction and after an hour of being near the horse, it seems unlikely that she's sensitive to it.

"I can't believe how quickly Cora's learning to ride it," Ms. Pierce exclaims. "I would have never thought to even try it. I'm so glad that Lisa invited us!"

Sam and Cora's mom are sitting next to each other on a large hay bale in the barn, watching the riders in the adjacent field. After walking alongside her daughter for fifteen minutes, Cassy took over to give Kendra a break. Lisa is now leading the mare while Ally and her mom prance around on two of the bigger horses.

"Cora doesn't seem to be allergic at all!" Sam observes. Looking sideways at the older woman, she watches her nod in agreement and then takes the opportunity to expand on the topic. "Are her allergies mostly to dogs and cats, then?"

Pursing her lips, Kendra clasps her hands tightly in her lap before turning to face Sam. "Yes, Sam. Dogs seem to be the worst." Pausing, she watches Cora for a minute before continuing. "I think that maybe you and I need to talk."

Sam leans forward eagerly. "Sure, Ms. Pierce. We can talk."

"First, you need to call me Kendra. You make me feel a lot older than I am with all the formalities."

Smiling, Sam relaxes a little. "I'm sorry if I startled you at the lab on Friday. I have to admit that I *was* exploring a little and I probably shouldn't have been down that hallway."

"What were you doing there, Sam?"

Growing cautious, Sam's smile falters slightly.

While Kendra's tone isn't accusatory, it isn't exactly friendly, either. "Like I said then, John has a school assignment and he chose the lab to write about." Even to Sam's ears, the excuse sounds rather lame.

"Uh-huh," Kendra breathes, clearly getting frustrated. "Now why don't you tell me the *real* reason?"

Sam hesitates, staring down at a piece of hay poking her leg. Pulling at it, she then begins to wrap the long brown straw around her finger. "John really is writing a paper," she begins. "But you're right, that wasn't the main reason I was there."

Tossing the balled up hay out into the field, Sam gathers up her courage and faces Kendra. "Ally, Cassy, and I have been volunteering at the local animal shelter. Three stray dogs were brought in during the same week, all with identical weird allergy symptoms."

Sam didn't know what she expected, but the change in Kendra is dramatic. The color draining from her face, she suddenly jumps off the hay bale. Wrapping her arms around herself, she starts pacing in front of Sam.

"What did these dogs look like?" she finally asks, almost whispering.

"Ummm .... Well, one was a white Bichon, a Schnauzer, and a Miniature Poodle."

Shoulders sagging, Kendra sits back down again, looking dejected. "You're a smart girl, Sam."

Sam squirms restlessly, unsure of how to take the compliment and waits for Kendra to continue. Staring out at the field, she watches the horses and wonders how much longer the riders will be able to handle the chilly morning air.

"How much did you see at the lab?"

Surprised by the question, Sam answers carefully. "I'm not sure what you mean, but I didn't see anything other than what I guess I'd expect. A bunch of machines and equipment that I have no clue what they are or what they do."

When Kendra doesn't respond, Sam suspects that she isn't going to tell her more than she has to, so she decides to get to the point. "It's more like what I *heard*. Coming from the room that I saw you walking out of. A dog barking. Why is there a dog there, Kendra?"

Sighing, Kendra places her hands over her

face, as if to block out the question. Shaking her head, she drops them back into her lap and then finally faces Sam. "It's not what you think. I would have never -- ,"

Before Kendra can finish, Sam's cell phone rings. Irritated by the interruption, she looks down at the caller ID and is surprised to see the shelter number. Maybe it got busy, and they need to girls to come in? Giving Kendra an apologetic smile, she answers on the fourth ring.

"Hello?"

"Sam? It's Pauline. Can you talk?"

A sudden sense of doom engulfs Sam and her mouth goes dry, making it difficult to answer. She already knows what Pauline is going to tell her. "Sure," she manages to say, her throat tight.

"I'm sorry, Sam, but I thought you'd want to know. Someone just came in and claimed to be Rocky's owners. He's gone."

14

IT'S ALL IN THE DE-TAILS

"You *have* to help me get him back!" Sam pleads. She's done talking in riddles. If Kendra knows something and can help them save the dogs, then she needs to do the right thing.

"The last dog at the kennel," Kendra replies. The fact that she already seems to know what Sam is talking about confirms her involvement.

"The cinnamon-colored poodle," Sam chokes out, her welling emotions threatening to overwhelm her. "You know, that one that was missing patches of hair and had his eyes all red and swollen because of whatever *you* were torturing him with!" Sam's anger startles her, and she slaps a hand over her mouth. She never talks to adults that way, but her love and concern for Rocky is taking over.

"I'm sorry, Sam," Kendra gasps, her eyes wide. Shaking her head, she approaches her and gently takes her by the shoulders. "You have to believe me. I had no idea what was going on. I tried to help them," she adds, backing away. "I'm the one that let them go."

Pausing, Sam swallows hard. Kendra might be telling the truth. Aware that Lisa or Ally's mom could come over at any minute, Sam realizes that any chance of getting answers would be lost. Kendra might not be so willing to speak with other adults about her involvement. If it's illegal, it could mean at the least her job, and maybe worse. Glancing over at Cora, still laughing on the back of the horse, Sam's anger turns to apprehension. Kendra might really be into some trouble.

Reaching out, Sam rests a hand on Kendra's arm and guides her back over to the hay bales. "Will you tell me what's going on, then?" she asks, careful to keep her voice level and free of emotion. "Maybe the director at the animal shelter can help. I'm sure that if you've tried to do the right thing, no one will blame you."

"I'm not so sure," Kendra counters. Sitting on her hands, she stares down at her new-looking cowboy boots. "It all started a couple of months ago. At first, Ted told me that the lab was invited to take part in a new trial that a large pharmaceutical was developing. It was exciting."

"Ted?" Sam asks, mulling over the information.

"Oh! You probably know him as Mr. Clancy. He's been running the lab ever since Mr. Carpenter started it. I didn't even think to question him, or the motives behind the labs involvement. Besides, we were only supposed to be participating in a very small way. It was two-fold. First, we were creating the base compound for the cream, and then we were going to run some tests on the proteins in it."

Sam is already getting a little lost, but she simply nods at Kendra, trying to encourage her to continue.

"I should have known that the lack of details for the testing phase was suspicious. We aren't set up for that sort of thing, really. But when you're given a chance to further your career and your boss is saying it's legit, you don't doubt it.

"At first, it was all good. We were ahead of schedule for the base and we all got a nice bonus check. But then -- " Pausing, she looks at Sam. Her blue eyes are red again, but this time it's from tears rather than allergies. "The dogs showed up. Ted said that the permits were all arranged through the larger corporation. I wasn't directly involved with them, so it was several days later before I saw the animals again. By then, it was apparent that they were testing the product on the dogs. It wasn't going well."

"What about Mr. Carpenter?" Sam questions, her heart rate picking up at the description of what was being done to poor Rocky and the other dogs.

"He's got *no* idea!" Kendra exclaims. Her frustration is clearly growing. "His wife has gotten much worse. For the last six months, he only comes to the lab once a month for a regular meeting where Ted goes through everything with him. When he showed up a few weeks ago, the dogs disappeared for the day. I of course expected the new project to be discussed at length with Mr. Carpenter. When Ted didn't even mention it, I knew things were way off. I tried to corner Ted afterwards and he made it painfully clear that if I valued my job, I wouldn't press the issue. He also pointed out that if I tried to report the animal testing to the USDA, that Mr. Carpenter would be the one to suffer the greatest loss. Sam, Ted said that he would testify that I was a key part of it from the beginning."

Tears spilling onto her cheeks, Kendra fights to keep her composure. "I didn't know what else to do, other than let the dogs go. I'm sure Ted figures that I did it, and his silence about it scares me even more. I don't know what he'd do if I tried to expose the program now."

"What *is* the program?" Sam asks, remembering Ally's suspicion from Friday night. "I mean, I know that it has to be some sort of allergy medicine, but why do they need the dogs?"

"Because the medication they're making is *for* dogs, not people," Kendra explains. "It would be a revolutionary creation. That's why I was so excited to be working on it. You see, they suspect that the main allergen is a protein that's excreted in the dog's saliva. That it's then transferred to the hair and skin through licking and then when the hair is shed, the allergen is released. That might be why non-shedding dogs are sometimes better tolerated by people who are allergy-prone."

Sam already knows most of this, but she didn't know about the proteins. She still doesn't really understand what that is, but the way that Kendra describes it makes sense. *I really need to pay more attention in science class,* Sam thinks.

"I guess they chose the more hypo-allergenic breeds to use as a sort of control. You see, no one is really a hundred percent sure about all of this allergy stuff, Sam. Whether at all comes down to the saliva, the skin, the hair, or some other factor. This cream acts as a protein-blocking compound. When used on the dog, the idea is that it prevents the allergen from absorbing into the hair or skin, making it truly hypoallergenic. This would be an amazing breakthrough, especially for suffers like Cora and me. I think that was one of the reasons Ted had me brought in on that phase. He was using *me* as a test subject, in a way."

"But you were all allergic when you came to

pick Cora up, and Cora had a bad reaction to your lab coat," Sam points out.

"That's because they also brought in some dogs that shed," Kendra says quietly.

"You mean there's *more?*" Sam moans, picturing a room full of cages.

"Just two German Shepherds," Kendra answers quickly. "When things started off badly with the first batch of dogs and I let them go, Ted immediately had the two shedding dogs brought in. I don't really know what they're doing with them now. My involvement was limited to begin with, but I was shut out after I questioned things. When you saw me coming out of the room Friday, you scared me so badly because I wasn't supposed to be in there."

"What were you doing?" Sam asks. A louder peel of laughter draws Sam's attention and she looks to where Lisa is helping Cora off the horse on the other side of the field. They'll be making their way over to them soon and time is running out.

"I was taking pictures of the dogs with my cell phone," Kendra admits. "I've been trying to figure out a way to stop this without bankrupting

Mr. Carpenter and losing everything. I know it might sound selfish, Sam, but I'm all Cora has."

Sam's chest aches at the thought of Kendra and Cora losing their home and everything else, because of what Ted has done. Kendra didn't know what they were doing and she's stuck in a horrible position now that she does.

"Do you really believe the director at the shelter can help, if I were to get her the information and proof?" Kendra asks. "I think that I can get copies of the original documents and contract from the other lab, and it would prove that Mr. Carpenter was never involved."

Her hopes rising, Sam thinks back over the conversation with Trish. She certainly understood the laws and said she'd been involved in it before. If she has a way of knowing who's applied for the permits to do animal testing, than she probably has a way to report them, too. If nothing else, she could at least pass the information on to the right people and then hopefully help get the dogs out right away.

"I'm sure she can do *something,* Kendra," Sam promises. "I totally get why you've been afraid to say anything to anyone," she adds. "But why didn't you just go and talk to Mr. Carpenter as soon you realized he didn't know? Won't he just shut it down and fire Ted?"

Shaking her head, Kendra starts acting nervous again. "I don't think it's that easy," she says, glancing at her daughter and the rest of the group now walking towards them. "The people in charge of this whole thing? I'm not sure who they are, but I can tell that Ted is afraid of them. I don't know what would happen if Mr. Carpenter tried to step in. He has so much going on with his wife that I couldn't bring myself to drop this on him. Honestly, he doesn't care about the company right now and I don't blame him. I think the best way to keep him safe in all of this is to not involve him."

"Well, what about you and Cora?" Sam asks, realizing suddenly that this might be dangerous for more than just the dogs. She hadn't even considered that possibility.

"That's why I haven't told anyone yet," Kendra whispers. "And I wouldn't be telling you any of this, either, but when I saw you there on Friday, I knew that you were getting dangerously close. Too close."

Lisa calls out a greeting as they approach and Sam waves back, doing her best to smile normally.

Glancing at her watch, Kendra then stands up and brushes off her jeans. "I'm dropping Cora off now at her Grandmas for the afternoon. No one will be at the lab on a Sunday. I've been gathering some stuff already in addition to the pictures. I'll stop by, grab it, and look for the contract and some other things. If I can't find what I need, then I'll go to Mr. Carpenter. I certainly won't involve you beyond delivering the papers anonymously for me. Can you meet me at my house at three? If you can get to the director today, maybe she can figure out a way to get Rocky back for you."

Any thought of danger is pushed aside at the mention of Rocky, and Sam finds herself nodding eagerly as Cora runs up to give her mom a hug.

15

WHEN PLANS GO AWRY

"I still think that we should call the police or tell my mom," Ally states, placing her hands on her hips. She's straddling her bike, in the middle of the group.

After Kendra and Cora left the farm, the rest of them stayed behind to help groom the horses and muck the stalls. Sam didn't have a chance to tell them about the conversation until after they got back home, less than half an hour ago.

Sam was relived to discover that the boys were both at Ally's house and she quickly suggested that they all go for a bike ride, which isn't unusual. She filled them all in on the plan once they stopped at the end of the road.

"I agree that we need to get an adult involved," John says to his sister. "But the police won't do anything. It's not like they've broken any laws or city ordinances. I think it's a federal business regulation or something. I doubt that anyone would even go to jail over it if they're found guilty, they'll just have to pay fines."

"We *are* going to involve an adult," Sam urges. "I already texted Trish and told her we're going to stop by in a little while. After we give her the evidence, I'll talk to my mom. I'm sure once she hears about this she'll want to help Rocky. What about the animal police?" Sam rushes on, before John can pick her strategy apart. "I've seen shows on TV about them and how they go rescue animals and stuff."

"Ha!" Hunter chortles. "You *really* think Oceanside has animal police? The whole police force has like, three cops. The Chief would probably roll his eyes at you and tell you to mind your own business."

"Okay then, Einstein," Sam counters. "What do you think we should do?"

"I say we just go in there and get the dogs."

Sam stares at her brother in shock. It's the last thing she expected him to say.

"Hunter, there's all sorts of reasons why we can't do that!" John nearly yells. "One big one would be trespassing. Oh, and stealing! Which, by the way, *is* against the law and something we could be arrested for."

"Relax," Hunter says, holding his hands out at John. "I didn't say anything about breaking into the place. But if Kendra was to let the dogs go like she did before, we could just happen to be out on a ride and find some strays."

While Sam is tempted to side with her brother, she knows that John is right. It would be wrong for them to get involved that way. She realizes now that Hunter must really like Rocky, too.

"They'd just get more dogs," Cassy says reasonably.

"I think that I was wrong before," John admits. His tone has changed, and his brows are drawn together in a severe frown. "I should have gone and talked to Mr. Carpenter in the first place and avoided all of this. I still could."

"What if he already knows?"

Cassy's question hangs in the air between them and is something no one had considered.

"I know he was your teacher, John," Cassy says, breaking the silence. "But you can't know him that well. It's possible that either he's in on the whole thing, or maybe he's even blackmailed. The point is that we have no way of knowing and we could end up making things worse."

John runs his hands through his already messy blonde hair and purses his lips, letting his breath out slowly. His lack of an argument against the suggestion is enough for Sam.

"So, we stick with the original plan?" she asks, looking at each of her friends in turn.

When no one disagrees, Ally pulls out her phone to check the time. "It's nearly three," she announces. "We should head over to Kendra's place, if we're going."

Sam is the first to peddle away and after a tense moment, she hears the other four kids follow. Looking back, she breathes a huge sigh of relief. She wouldn't go through with it if they didn't all approve.

Kendra's driveway is empty when they arrive,

so they peddle around the side of the house and lean their bikes up against the detached garage in the backyard. Sam and Ally's houses are both visible from the front and neither one of them want to explain what they're doing there to their parents.

Sam feels a brief surge of guilt at the thought, knowing that the need to hide her actions is a sure sign that she probably shouldn't be doing it. But she counters it with the knowledge that it's only temporary. Once they have the proof they need to shut down the experiments, she can tell her mom everything. This is the only way she knows to make sure that Rocky is safe and right now, that's the most important thing to her.

Pacing with nervous energy, Sam's anxiety increases with each passing minute. Ally and Cassy join her march across the deck, while John and Hunter lounge on the patio furniture. After a long half-hour, the girls finally flop down on the remaining chairs.

"She isn't answering my text messages," Ally says nervously. "She's normally one of those people that will respond right away."

"Maybe her phone doesn't work inside the

lab?" Hunter suggests.

Shaking her head, Ally sends off another text. "No. The last few times I babysat, she was messaging me from inside the lab, telling me when she was going to leave."

"Maybe we *should* call the police now," Cassy states. "She could be in trouble."

"And tell them what, exactly?" Hunter challenges. "Maybe her phone died, or she lost it, or she left it back at the barn. Maybe she chickened out and is too embarrassed to tell you. There are a number of reasons why she might not be answering a text and we don't have any compelling reasons to interest the police in any of them."

"Let's go," Sam announces, jumping to her feet. "It should only take us ten minutes to ride our bikes out there. If we find her car in the parking lot and she still isn't answering her phone, then we'll call our parents and have them contact Mr. Carpenter or the police."

"Good idea," John agrees. "But we *don't* go inside," he adds, giving Hunter a playful shove as they get to their feet.

"Yes, sir!" Hunter laughs, dodging another

push.

Less than fifteen minutes later, they reach the remote lab, located in a wooded area on the outskirts of town. While it's not quite four in the afternoon, the sun has already begun its rapid descent, plunging the property into growing shadows. At first, Sam doesn't see Kendra's distinctive red sedan, but as they peddle around the backside of the parking lot, they locate it next to what looks like a loading dock.

Coming to a stop next to the empty car, Sam looks at Ally hopefully.

"The phones ringing," she explains, holding it out so they can all hear it. "So it isn't dead." Lowering it when Kendra's voicemail picks up, Ally hits the end button. "So? Want me to call my mom?"

"I'm sorry, Sam," John says, placing a hand on her shoulder. "I know you just want to get Rocky and the other dogs out, but I don't see what else we can do."

Her throat tightening again for the second time that day, Sam hangs her head in resignation. So much for a simple plan. "I know," she replies. "Go ahead and call, Ally. It's the -- "

Suddenly, a familiar barking erupts from near her head and Sam spins to discover Rocky standing on the loading dock!

"Rocky!" she cries, running towards him without even considering *how* he could be there.

"Sam, wait!" John shouts, making a grab for her arm but missing.

As she reaches the cement ramp, Rocky leaps towards her but suddenly pulls up short and gives a pitiful yelp. Confused, Sam falters and then realizes too late that he's on a leash. Holding the leash is Mr. Clancy.

"I'll take that phone." A deep voice demands.

Spinning back the other way, Sam discovers that two other men have walked up behind them.

"In fact," the bigger of the two continues, holding out a hand. "I'll take *all* your phones."

16

CAGED

Ally freezes, the cell phone clutched tightly in her hand. She was so focused on Rocky that she didn't even hear the men walking up around the car. Eying the one directing the order at her, she tries to measure the situation. They seem pretty serious.

"I don't like repeating myself," he growls, stepping closer to Ally.

"Hey!" John shouts, moving towards his sister. "Back off, man. We're just looking for our friend."

"You're trespassing, John," Mr. Clancy says coolly. "This is private property, and we aren't open for 'tours' today," he adds, scowling at Sam.

"We're in a parking lot," Hunter counters. He's doing his best to act laid back while trying to enter the password to unlock his phone. Sam always gives him a hard time for having such a long code.

"A parking lot that's behind a fence with signs that say don't enter," the larger man points out. Snatching the phone out of Ally's hand, he then takes another step towards John. "Now give me your phone, kid."

Though John is big for his age, he's still no match for the thug. Glancing briefly at his sister's startled face and then Cassy's wide, frightened eyes, John realizes that the wisest move is to try to diffuse the confrontation. "Okay, Okay," he placates, holding his hands out with the phone in a 'slow down' gesture. "I don't know why you're so uptight with us riding though here, but we didn't mean to cause you any grief. We'll leave, Mr. Clancy."

"Enough of the games," Mr. Clancy replies. "I've been reading the incoming text messages from 'Ally' for the past half-hour," he says, looking between Ally and Cassy, unsure of which one is the culprit. "I don't know why a bunch of kids are caught up in helping a disgruntled employee steal from me, and I don't like being lied to," he adds while looking at John. "But until we talk this over with your parents, I'll hold onto your phones. Craig, bring them up here. Let's all go inside and figure this out."

Sam's mind races as she watches her brother and friends ushered towards the loading dock. *Craig.* The name was familiar. *The animal shelter! Could it be the same guy that quit a couple of months ago?*

In spite of her knowledge that Mr. Clancy is doing something wrong and trying to shift the blame onto them, Sam still feels guilty over his accusation. The whole thing is a mess. If he succeeds in destroying all the evidence, could he get away with it? Moaning inwardly, Sam realizes how she set herself up already with Trish and her mom, to make it appear that she was once again over reacting and nosing around.

Craig finishes collecting Cassy and Hunter's phones as they reach her. Glancing at her bike laying nearby on the ground, Sam wonders how fast she could get to it. Would the men even try to stop her if she made a run for it? While they haven't exactly threatened them, it's clear that they don't want them to leave. And why would they? Mr. Clancy saw the texts, which means he found Kendra inside and knows they're working with her on proving what he's up to. She *could* run off and call her mom … but by the time her mom got here, the dogs might be long gone and Mr. Clancy will point out how the kids were trespassing and are the ones in the wrong. With her history for doing just that, it might all backfire.

Craig puts a hand out for her phone. Hesitating, Sam takes another fleeting look at her bike. John has come up behind her on the ramp and taking Sam's arm, he gives it a cautionary squeeze. He's probably already come to the same conclusion. Their best chance is to get inside with Kendra, find the dogs, and try to figure out how to rescue them.

"If you really want to talk with our parents, I'd be happy to call my mom for you." Slapping the phone into Craig's hand, Sam can't resist pointing out the obvious contradiction to the men taking their phones, but then turns and walks up the ramp.

Mr. Clancy glares at Sam in response, and

silently waves them all in through the big delivery doors. Inside is a large receiving area that's full of boxes and various supplies.

Standing in the middle of the room is Kendra. Her shoulders are slumped and she's holding a manila envelope in one hand. A small cardboard box is cradled in her other arm. Her distraught expression turns to a mixture of defeat and anger when she sees the kids.

A tall, skinny man is pacing the floor behind Kendra and he nearly erupts when the group enters. "Awww, come on!" he whines, throwing his arms up in exasperation. "You said this was going to be simple, Ted. My employer likes simple. He doesn't like complicated. If things get too complicated, we just go somewhere else for business."

"Nothing's changed," Mr. Clancy assures him. "Your product is right there, ready to load up," he explains, pointing at one of the nearby stacks of boxes. "Phillip is going to bring it around to your van now.'

The other man that was outside with them rushes to follow the order. While not as muscular as Craig, the middle-aged man has no problem carrying and stacking three of the boxes at a time onto a dolly.

Watching him move, Sam suddenly realizes Kendra's horrible timing. While there normally wouldn't be anyone in the building on a Sunday, Mr. Clancy chose to deliver the final product now, for the same reason. She can only imagine what a horrible scene it must have been when Kendra was caught with the company files and whatever other proof was in the box.

"This is all just a misunderstanding," Mr. Clancy says while gesturing first at Kendra and then the kids. "My employee here grew too much of a conscience, but she's smart enough to look out for her own best interest."

"And the brats?" the buyer demands, still not looking convinced.

"Just some disillusioned kids that are about to find out how the laws really work." Mr. Clancy hands Rocky's leash to Craig. "Get him in the cage with the others."

Sam's heart speeds up when she sees where Craig is leading the poodle. On the far side of the storage area, several cages are stacked on a forklift, ready to be moved. Inside them are the two other dogs from the shelter, plus the German Shepherds Kendra told her about.

Walking over to Kendra, Ted Clancy snatches the folder and box from her hands. "Take these, too," he says, handing the items off to Craig. "It can all disappear together."

"Ted, please," Kendra begs. Her face is pale and her hands are trembling, but she still takes a step towards her boss. "I'm just trying to do what's right. I thought you were best friends with Mr. Carpenter. You know he'd be devastated if he knew about this!"

"Which is why he'll never know," Ted says evenly. "My pal is a great man, but not a good businessman. When this is all over, I'll be able to buy this place from him and run things the *right* way."

"I won't let you," Kendra declares, her eyes flashing.

"You know," Ted says coyly. "You have a little girl to take care of. Remember that you're involved in this, too." Pointing at her chest, the man leans in close and lowers his voice to a menacing purr. "If any of this gets turned over to the USDA, I'll see to it that you not only lose your job, but that you *never* work in this field of study again!"

Her skin paling even more, Kendra staggers back several steps as if physically hit.

"Look, just give us the dogs and none of us will say anything about the other stuff," Sam pleads. Although coming here and collecting the evidence was Kendra's idea, Sam knows that she probably wouldn't have done it if Sam hadn't questioned her. This could all be *her* fault.

"Oh, I *know* you aren't going to say anything," Ted agrees. "Because if you do, I'll see to it that Kendra loses much more than just her job and all of you will get a trespassing and burglary charge!"

Sam looks at John, hoping that he'll challenge Ted and tell him it'll never work. But instead, he shakes his head at her solemnly. Sam remembers how John told her two weeks ago to let this go, and she feels even worse. Ally steps up to her side and loops an arm through hers in a gesture of support and she leans against her friend.

Hunter and Cassy are sitting together on a large crate. While Cassy is staring dismally at the floor, Hunter has his legs stuck out and crossed at the ankles, with his arms folded across his chest. He's doing his best to appear bored and disinterested, but Sam knows her brother. He's waiting for an opportunity to make a scene the first chance he gets.

The only way out of this without them or Kendra getting into trouble is to have proof, and Ted is making sure that none of it remains. That it all 'disappears'. Including the dogs.

Rocky.

He's their proof, and Craig is about to put him in the last empty cage. Where will they take him? What are they going to do with the dogs to make them *disappear*? The possible answers to those questions are enough to compel Sam to take action. She doesn't care if she's the one to get into trouble. He *has* to get away.

"Rocky!" Sam suddenly yells, lunging towards him. "Rocky! Run!"

About to latch the cage, Craig has dropped the leash and is unprepared for the dog's reaction. Charging at the door, Rocky knocks it out of Craig's grasp and then slips through the opening. He hits the floor running and heads straight for Sam!

"No, Rocky!" Sam screams. Pointing at the still-open delivery doors, she dives sideways to avoid Ted. "Go outside! Outside!"

The room erupts into chaos as all of the dogs begin barking and Craig runs after the loose poodle. Hunter leaps from the crate and makes a dash for the papers and box that fell from Craig's hands.

For a moment, Sam thinks she might actually reach the doors with Rocky when suddenly; she's wrapped up from behind. Strong arms engulf her and she's lifted off her feet!

"You're going to regret that!" Ted snarls in her ear.

Before Sam has a chance to react, Rocky is there and leaping at her attacker, knocking them all to the ground. With a viciousness she didn't think the loving dog was capable of, he latches onto Ted's leg and growls around the fabric in his mouth.

Finding herself released and unhurt, Sam rolls away and staggers to her feet. The open doors are right in front of her and she literally falls through them, hoping that her friends are right behind.

But instead of a clear loading dock and a path to freedom, Sam slams into something solid. Dazed, she falls back and then looks up, cringing at the burning anger on Trish's face.

17

UNEXPECTED ALLIANCE

"Trish!" Sam gasps.

Trish reaches out and grabs ahold of Sam's arms to prevent her from falling down. Her scowl deepens as she swings her head around, trying to take in the confusing scene. "Craig!" she bellows when she spots her former employee. "What are *you* doing here?"

"I work here," he says with trepidation. He's gotten Rocky off Mr. Clancy's leg and has a firm grasp on the leash. He managed to drag the dog back several feet, but froze when he saw Trish.

"What?" Tilting her head at him, Trish purses her lips.

Sam can almost see the pieces coming

together in Trish's intelligent eyes. She's relieved that Trish isn't involved in the illegal animal testing, but has no idea what she can do to help. Releasing Sam, the intimidating woman then takes a step towards Craig.

"I thought you were working at the shelter over in Fulton County," She asks suspiciously. Looking down at Ted, Trish then glances at the other kids huddled together before focusing her attention on the cages.

"I was," Craig answers. Pulling harder at the leash, he continues to back away slowly. "But it was only temporary. Did you really think I was going to use my Biology major and Chemistry sub-major to clean stinkin *animals*?"

"I get it," Trish answers matter-of-factly. "You used the job to collect strays from another county. It might have worked out better if you didn't lose them," she adds, her contempt for the man now apparent. "But you never were very good with the animals."

"This is a touching reunion and all," Ted states. Standing now, he brushes off his pants and straightens his lab coat. "But I'm going to have to ask you to leave," he says to Trish.

"You're trespassing and this is none of your business."

"Ted Clancy," Trish declares, unmoved by his demand. "I thought that Baby was a house pet." Nodding towards the cages and the small white dog, her face reddens. "Tell ya what. I'll take those dogs off your hands and the kids and I will be happy to go."

"I'm out of here!" the tall, whiny man interrupts. "I'm simply picking up an order that's part of a legal contract between my employer and Mr. Clancy. Anything else going on, including whether he conducted his own business appropriately or not, has nothing to do with me!"

Waving at Phillip, who is still standing by a now fully loaded flat dolly, he motions for him to follow. No one attempts to stop them as the two make their way past Trish and onto the loading dock. "I think it's safe to say that we'll be severing any future partnership," he adds pausing to look at Ted. "But we'll be in touch."

Ted's face darkens and he spins on Kendra. "This is all *your* doing! You haven't a clue what this meant for the company. The amount of money involved is more than you'll see in your lifetime and more than enough to get the proper medical care for Mrs. Carpenter."

"It isn't your place to involve Mr. Carpenter's business in something without his knowledge," Kendra counters. "I have a feeling that if he *was* involved, it would be done the right way. That might not mean as much money for *you*, and it would take longer, but it would be something we could all actually be proud of."

Laughing in a crazy, high shrilling voice, Ted motions to Craig. "Come on! We've got work to do, and we'll have to set up a meeting with the corporation. It's time we went into business for ourselves. Grab that!" he continues, pointing at the items that Hunter's clutching tightly.

"Craig, I wouldn't do that." Trish's voice has taken on a different quality, and Sam is suddenly very glad to have the older woman by her side.

"Why are you still here?" Ted demands, turning back to Trish. "Get off this property, and don't come back!"

"I'm going to say this one more time," Trish counters, unfazed. "Those dogs were in my care and I released them to you under false pretenses. I'm quite certain that if I were to call the shelter in Fulton County, they'd say the same thing about the Shepherds. So I'm taking them back. I'm leaving with them and the kids are coming with me! Be careful how you answer," she warns, pointing at Ted. "As it is, you might just be looking at some fines for not having proper permits for the work you're conducting. But I get the feeling that you're dangerously close to crossing a line here. I won't hesitate to call the police and we can let them determine if other, more serious charges are appropriate."

His face turning an even darker shade of red, Ted studies Trish briefly before walking over to Craig. Grabbing the cell phones from him, he then approaches John. "Here, kid," he growls, dumping them in his hands. "I hope you realize what you're about to do to Mr. Carpenter."

"You mean what *you* did." Stuffing the cells in his pockets, John stares at the man that could have been his mentor. He realizes now that ignoring something that's wrong simply because it makes you uncomfortable will only lead to bigger problems. He should have spoken with his teacher right away. Doing the right thing isn't always easy.

"Get out!" Ted yells at everyone in the room. "Take the mutts with you."

Sam runs forward to Rocky, her chest welling with emotion. Snatching the leash from a scowling Craig, she doesn't stop to pet him now. Leading him over to the cages, she joins Cassy and Ally. They've already got Baby out and are working on the others.

Less than five minutes later, they have all five dogs out in the parking out and Trish is leading them towards the shelter's van. Kendra and Hunter are the only ones not holding a leash, and Hunter gives her the folder and box back.

"Thank you," Kendra tells him, holding the items close. "I'm taking this straight to Mr. Carpenter," she says, turning to Sam. "I should have done it weeks ago."

"Do you really think he's going to lose the lab over this?" Sam worries, looking from Kendra to Trish.

"Here," Trish replies, reaching into a back pocket. "Kendra is your name?" When Kendra nods, she hands her a business card. "After you speak to this Mr. Carpenter, have him call me. I can put him in contact with the appropriate authorities. If he really has no idea that this is happening, and you can testify to that, I don't see why he'd be the one to be charged with anything."

"These papers will prove that," Kendra assures everyone, holding up the folder. "It includes the contract, and the only name on it is Ted Clancy's."

Smiling now, Sam kneels down to hug Rocky. The poodle licks her face affectionately before resting his head on her shoulder in a doggy embrace.

18

SHELTERED IN LOVE

The ride to the shelter is brief, and with the dogs all clambering around the back of the van, there is little conversation. Sam is relieved to escape the noisy vehicle and leads them all in through the front door.

"Oh, my gosh!" Pauline shouts when she sees them. "What in the world happened? Where were you, and why do you have all these dogs?"

"I'll explain everything," Trish laughs, handing over the Shepherds to Pauline. "But first, you need to call your mom, Sam!"

Sam's joy fades a little.

"When you didn't show up here for the meeting you arranged with me, I got worried. So,

I called your mom. Apparently, she didn't know you were planning on coming here this afternoon. When I told her that Rocky was adopted out, she got very quiet and then said that the last she saw you, you were going on a bike ride with all of your friends."

Sam exchanges a knowing look with Ally. Too many times, they've found themselves in this same position, of having to defend their actions to their parents. It often ends in some sort of lecture, grounding, and the threat to never let them leave the house again.

"She tried calling you on your cell – and then tried *all* of you. When no one answered, she said she was going to go looking."

Moaning, Hunter slaps his forehead. "Man, we're going to get it bad for this one."

"How did you find us?" Sam asks, while getting her phone from John.

"I asked Pauline what you said to her when she called you earlier today about Rocky. What concerned me was what you *didn't* say!" Sam gives her a quizzical look, and Trish Smiles back at her. "You didn't ask *who* took him, Sam. So I figured it was because you thought you already knew. It wasn't hard at that point to conclude that you might go to the labs, where you believed he was, and try to get him back. I have to admit that I had no idea what I was going to be walking into when I got there!"

"Trish, what did you walk into?" Pauline demands, still in the dark.

While Trish tells the whole story to Pauline, Sam makes the dreaded call to her mom. Luckily, she mostly seems relieved when Sam tells her that they're all at the shelter with Trish. Rather than go into details on the phone, she promises to explain everything when they get there to pick them up.

"Our moms are on their way," Sam announces, turning back to the group.

"My mom, too?" Ally gasps, her eyes going wide.

"Yup. And Lisa. I guess they were all out searching for us together." Sam looks apologetically at Cassy, and then John. "Sorry, guys."

Shrugging, Cassy continues to pet Baby. "It's all good. The dogs are safe. I can handle a couple of weeks without TV."

"It's more than that," John counters. "It's about trust, and we just destroyed some of it. It's going to take some time to gain it back."

Sam knows that John is right. They might have had good intentions, but it was still unfair to their parents.

"Well, I can't help but feel that I'm partly to blame for this," Trish confides.

Surprised by the statement, Sam looks up from in between Rockies fluffy ears, where she was giving him another kiss. Pauline has gone to put the two German Shepherds into kennels, leaving the three other smaller dogs with them.

"You tried to do the right thing by involving an adult in your suspicions, but I didn't want to listen to it." Walking over to Sam, Trish kneels down so that she can pet Rocky. "I allowed the need for money to cloud my judgement, Sam. Ted Clancy was offering up a nice sum, for the 'return' of his supposed beloved pet. I wonder that if it weren't for that, would I have been more willing to listen?"

"The only one to blame for this is Mr. Clancy," Ally insists. "Besides, if it weren't for you, we probably wouldn't have gotten the dogs back!"

The phone rings, interrupting the conversation, and Trish goes to answer it. Sam watches Pauline return to take one small dog under each arm, leaving Rocky for last. Sam's growing dread of having to leave him there continues to mount and when headlights flash outside the window, she knows that time is about to run out.

Several minutes later the front door jingles and Sam's younger twin sisters erupt inside, followed by Lisa, Kathy, and Elizabeth. The adult's expressions are a mixture of relief and anger but fortunately, Trish gets off the phone just in time to intervene.

"Great news!" Trish announces, gesturing for them all to take a seat in the front waiting area. "I was on the phone with Mr. Carpenter, the owner of the lab," she explains to their parents. When it's clear that not everyone present knows who either Mr. Carpenter is, or what lab she's talking about, Trish graciously launches into a detailed explanation.

Sam listens intently, cringing each time her mom casts a furtive glance her way. The twins of course made a beeline for Rocky and are now jostling each other for the dog's attention. He's patiently allowing them to pet and hug him, only pulling away slightly when they begin to tug on his ears before Sam can stop them.

Trish does an amazing job of outlining what happened, very effectively casting the blame onto Ted Clancy and even herself, rather than the kids. When Lisa interrupts to remind Sam that she cautioned her early on about not confiding in adults in such matters, Trish admits that Sam tried. By the time she's done, Sam is actually hopeful that they could avoid any major groundings, but knows that there are still going to be consequences.

"Thank you for everything you've done," Kathy Wolf says to Trish. "It sounds like it could have possibly been a dangerous situation if you hadn't shown up."

"I agree,' Elizabeth Parker says, nodding. "I would like to talk with the police about it, actually. For no other reason, I want what Ted Clancy did to be on record, in an official report."

"Oh, Mr. Carpenter is contacting them now about it." Trish assures them. "I advised him to.

They should be calling each of you either tonight or tomorrow to give a written statement."

"Good," Lisa agrees. "And we'll be having a long conversation about whether you're ready for the responsibility that comes with volunteering here," she directs to Cassy. "Because right now, I'm not so sure."

"I certainly hope that you'll all allow the kids to come by and help." Trish stands and gestures to include the whole building. "This place might not be much, but it's all these animals have, and we get hundreds a year coming through."

"We'd like to start volunteering, too." It's the first thing John has said since his mom arrived, and she looks at him questioningly. "Me and Hunter," he adds. When Hunter gives him a look, John waves at him to be quiet. "Think of it as part of our punishment," he suggests, and Hunter gives him a small, knowing smile.

"I'd be happy to have you," Trish tells John, smiling broadly.

"What was the great news?" Ally asks, reminding Trish of her initial declaration when she first got off the phone.

"Oh, yes! Well, Kendra is there with Mr.

Carpenter now, and I of course validated everything I could. Based on the documents Kendra brought him, he's firing Ted Clancy immediately and making Kendra Pierce the new director of operations!"

"That's wonderful!" Ally says, wrapping an arm around Sam. She'd been so concerned about Cora's mom, and now her job is going to be even better!

"And …," Trish continues. "In exchange for my helping him with the process of reporting the animal abuse, and to make up for what happened, he wants to be an active donor to the shelter. He believes that legally, he owns the rights to the new allergy cream that was created. He wants to go the proper route with its development and do it without testing on animals. It could be worth a whole lot of money! With the amount of funding he's talking about, I'll be able to hire the other employee I need, and expand our services!" Turning to Pauline, Trish reaches out to take her hand. "I'll also be able to pay you what you deserve. I value everything you do here and I want to make sure you're successful with your schooling!"

Her features softening, Lisa goes to Cassy and gives her younger sister a big hug. "You can continue to volunteer," she says, holding her at arm's length. "But you really scared me today. Don't do it again, okay? Next time, tell me what's going on."

Cassy hugs her back, and nods silently. It's been less than six months since they've been in each other's lives, and she already can't imagine what it would be like without her sister. Although they were raised separately, without any knowledge of the other's existence, they were both orphaned at a young age. Cassy knows that Lisa loves her and only wants her to be safe.

"I'm starving."

Sam looks irritably at her brother. Leave it to him to break up an emotional moment. To her surprise, he approaches her and leans down to take Rocky from her lap. Her first thought is that he has the nerve to hand him off to Pauline, in order to speed up their departure. However, he instead holds the poodle close and walks up to their mom.

"Meet Rocky," he says simply, and places the dog in her arms.

Just as startled as Sam is surprised by her brother's off-handed support, Kathy holds the medium-sized dog a bit awkwardly. It isn't that she doesn't like pets, but with four kids in the house, including two-year-old twins, it isn't very feasible.

Rocky seems to understand the gravity of the meeting, and he stops squirming so that he can stare into her eyes. Kathy looks back, and the dog holds her gaze for so long, that she finds it impossible to turn away. Then, chuffing once, the poodle leans forward and gently presses his nose against her forehead. Laughing, Kathy smiles at him, but doesn't resist when Pauline offers to take him.

"I think what we all need is food," Elizabeth states, filling the uneasy silence. "If no one is opposed to pizza, there's plenty of room at our house, and there's toys in the rec room for the twins."

Sam slowly gets to her feet with the help of Ally and Cassy. Looking at her two best friends, she does her best not to tear up. Watching Pauline turn to leave the room with Rocky, she forces herself to follow everyone else to the front door. But when she reaches it, her mom puts out a hand to stop her.

"Aren't you forgetting something, young lady?"

Staring back at her mom, Sam's confusion grows. Though her voice is stern, her expression is warm.

"You never leave a friend behind."

Her heart feels like it might explode as Sam throws her arms around her mom. "Really?" she whispers, her vision blurring. "Do you mean it?"

Smiling now, Kathy points at Rocky, where Pauline has set him down on the floor. "Go get him."

Feeling as if she's in a dream, Sam runs to the poodle that has come to mean so much to her. Pulling him into her arms, she makes a silent promise to always love and protect him. As her friends gather around, she looks up at them, knowing that they would do the same for her.

"Come on," she tells Rocky, staring into his big, gentle eyes. "Let's go home."

THE END

Thank you for reading, *'The Case of the Curious Canine!* I hope that you enjoyed it, and will take the time to write a simple review on Amazon!

Be on the lookout for more exciting adventures, and be sure to sign up for Tara Ellis's newsletter to get special offers. You can find the link for the newsletter and a complete list of books at her website on Amazon.

ABOUT THE AUTHOR

Author Tara Ellis lives in a small town in beautiful Washington State, in the Pacific Northwest. She enjoys the quiet lifestyle with her two teenage kids, and several dogs. Tara was a firefighter/EMT, and worked in the medical field for many years. She now concentrates on family, photography, and writing middle grade and young adult novels.

Visit her author page on Amazon to find all of her books!

Made in the USA
Monee, IL
19 July 2020